**Like a lamp switched on, Jordan
brightened immediately. "You mean
I'm not fired?"**

"Of course not."

"But what I said at the restaurant—"

"Was no reason for you to lose your job." Before
Jordan could respond too enthusiastically, Landry
raised a warning hand. "But we do need to set some
boundaries."

"Why?"

That wasn't the response Landry had expected.
"Because I am your employer." That was obvious
enough, wasn't it?

"Not because you're not attracted to me?"

It took a few moments for Landry to sort out the
question and craft an answer. "Whether I'm attracted
to you is irrelevant. I'm your—"

"My employer. Right. But it's still totally relevant."
Jordan tossed the clothing onto the nearest chair and
moved a step closer to Landry. "So *are* you? Attracted,
I mean?"

WELCOME TO

Dear Reader,

Love is the dream. It dazzles us, makes us stronger, and brings us to our knees. Dreamspun Desires tell stories of love featuring your favorite heartwarming heroes, captivating plots, and exotic locations. Stories that make your breath catch and your imagination soar.

In the pages of these wonderful love stories, readers can escape to a world where love conquers all, the tenderness of a first kiss sweeps you away, and your heart pounds at the sight of the one you love.

When you put it all together, you find romance in its truest form.

Love always finds a way.

Elizabeth North

Executive Director
Dreamspinner Press

Kim Fielding

REDESIGNING
LANDRY BISHOP

PUBLISHED BY

Published by
DREAMSPINNER PRESS

5032 Capital Circle SW, Suite 2, PMB# 279,
Tallahassee, FL 32305-7886 USA
www.dreamspinnerpress.com

Redesigning Landry Bishop
© 2019 Kim Fielding.
Editorial Development by Sue Brown-Moore.

Cover Art
© 2019 Alexandria Corza.
http://www.seeingstatic.com/
Cover content is for illustrative purposes only and any person depicted
on the cover is a model.

Paperback ISBN: 978-1-64108-117-7
Digital ISBN: 978-1-64405-106-1
Library of Congress Control Number: 2018914535
Paperback published May 2019
v. 1.0

Printed in the United States of America
(∞)
This paper meets the requirements of
ANSI/NISO Z39.48-1992 (Permanence of Paper).

KIM FIELDING is pleased every time someone calls her eclectic. Her books span a variety of genres, but all include authentic voices and unconventional heroes. She's a Rainbow Award and SARA Emma Merritt winner, a LAMBDA finalist, and a two-time Foreword INDIE finalist. She has migrated back and forth across the western two-thirds of the United States and currently lives in California, where she long ago ran out of bookshelf space. She's a university professor who dreams of being able to travel and write full-time. She also dreams of having two teenagers who occasionally get off their phones, a husband who isn't obsessed with football, and a cat who doesn't wake her up at 4:00 a.m. Some dreams are more easily obtained than others.

Blogs: kfieldingwrites.com and www.goodreads.com/author/show/4105707.Kim_Fielding/blog

Facebook: www.facebook.com/KFieldingWrites

Email: kim@kfieldingwrites.com

Twitter: @KFieldingWrites

By Kim Fielding

Published by **DREAMSPINNER PRESS**
www.dreamspinnerpress.com

Chapter One

LANDRY Bishop had already checked his appearance in the backstage mirror, but now that the cameras were ready to roll, he couldn't help but resmooth his pumpkin-hued sport jacket and adjust his gray pocket square a few millimeters.

He loved his fans. And he loved Suzee for giving him this ongoing opportunity to visit her show. He watched as she walked the aisles and worked the crowd—her makeup impeccable, a burgundy dress bringing out the hints of red in her artfully styled curls. She was breathtakingly pulled together and a natural host.

He was lucky to be here. This was part of his dream come true. If only the dream didn't involve television cameras.

One final deep breath. *Act as though you'd rather do this than anything else.* Showtime.

Suzee glanced at him, caught his *Ready to go* gesture, and gave him a wink. She stepped onto her mark and stretched an arm toward the wings, and grasped his hand when he came onstage. "Landry Bishop, everyone!" She gave the studio audience her trademark wide grin, and when the wild applause died down, she asked, "What do you have for us today, Landry?" She gestured at the table in front of her, its contents hidden by a white cloth.

Landry faced the audience and echoed Suzee's smile. The stage lights prevented him from seeing individual faces, but that wasn't a problem as he played to the whole crowd. "Well, we all know what today is, right? It's hump day." He waggled his eyebrows and the audience roared. They always loved double entendres, even if the jokes were long past their sell-by date.

"Now, now," he chided, pretending offense. "I *meant* it's Wednesday. And I think for a lot of us, it's a hard day to get through. The weekend still feels so far away. Am I right, ladies?" Actually, Suzee's audience always had a few men sprinkled throughout. Most of them were boyfriends or husbands dragged in by their significant others, but Suzee also had a fair number of male fans. Landry had heard rumors that a few came to see him. His segments often focused on advice for women, but none of the men had ever complained.

After everyone had sufficiently lamented the middle of the week, he nodded. "Today I have a solution for making Wednesdays a little easier to swallow. And this tip might seem to apply only to people who work in offices and shops, but those of you who work at home suffer from midweek blues too, so you should all listen up."

Suzee came a step closer and briefly touched his shoulder. "I know just what you mean, Landry. I love my job—I'm the luckiest lady in LA! But sometimes Wednesdays can be hard to get through."

"Then you need to listen up too! The key to Wednesdays is to make them special. Make them something to look forward to. I know that's hard when you're super busy, but if we take just a little extra time and effort, it'll be worth it. And here's how we're going to do it—we're going to turn a boring lunch into an *event*!"

With a flourish, he pulled the cloth off the table. He'd practiced for almost an hour, making sure the fabric billowed just right and that nothing on the table was jostled. He was pleased it went off without a hitch.

The audience oohed and aahed over the reveal as video screens provided an overhead view of the table, set for two with Bernardaud china, Christofle silverware, Waterford glassware, and Matouk linens. Landry slipped a lighter from his pocket and touched the flame to the two slim tapers in crystal holders. He'd had to argue with Suzee's producer and stage manager about that one— fire codes, blah blah blah—but Suzee had battled on his side and won. The table was much more dramatic with the flickering little flames, especially as the stage lights dimmed to show them off.

"That's beautiful, Landry," Suzee enthused. "But can people really manage this during an office lunch?"

"Of course! Unlike what we have here, the settings don't have to be hugely expensive, although you don't want to go cheap. The key is that they be beautiful and special. Don't use them for anything but Wednesday lunch. It won't cost too much because you only have to buy service for one. Or two." He winked and the audience laughed.

"Okay, I get you. But you don't expect us to eat tuna salad sandwiches on these pretty plates, do you?"

"I wouldn't recommend tuna salad in the workplace at all, actually. Nobody wants to be exposed to fish breath all afternoon. Anyway, with a setting this pretty, the meal should be extra nice too."

Landry gestured toward the back of the set, where the stagehand came out right on cue, pushing a wheeled metal cart. This particular stagehand, Todd, had landed the job more for his good looks and bodybuilder physique than his on-set skills. As usual when he appeared, the ladies in the audience cheered and clapped. Todd waved at them as he settled the cart into place.

"*Thank* you," Landry said, camping it up a little. Todd was sweet and earnest, but he wasn't Landry's type. Plus, he was straight. But Todd never seemed to mind when Landry pretended to flirt, and honestly, Landry had the suspicion that if he were persuasive enough, Todd might decide he wasn't *entirely* straight. Landry didn't intend to test it.

After Todd left, Suzee hovered over the cart. "What have you brought for us today?"

In truth, Landry hadn't brought anything, but he had provided the show's cooks with recipes ahead of time. If the ladies in the audience and at home wanted to imagine Landry slaving over a hot stove on their behalf, he wasn't going to disappoint them.

"What I'm going for here is special, but still healthy and tasty. These are dishes you can get ready the night before, and some of them you can even prep over the weekend and freeze until you're ready for them." He pointed to each item as he described it: the kimchi grain bowl, the Thai-inspired noodle and vegetable salad, the open-faced ham and unsalted butter on thinly sliced rye, the quinoa with pears and butternut squash, the orzo chicken with avocado-lime dressing, the apple and almond-butter terrine.

"That's a pretty big lunch!" Suzee said with a laugh.

"It would be if you ate it all in one meal. But you'll want to choose just two or three items. Go ahead." He pointed at her plate.

She obediently picked up her dish and served herself a slice of terrine and a spoonful of quinoa. Landry took one of the ham sandwiches, a little noodle salad, and some kimchi grains. Then, as Suzee sat down in front of her food, he pulled a bottle of sparkling cider from the cart's bottom shelf and filled their glasses with a flourish. "Sadly, most workplaces frown on wine at lunch, so we'll have to make do."

Landry took the chair next to her. As the audience watched breathlessly, he and Suzee made a brief toast— "Santé!"—and then dug in. Delicately, of course.

"Wow, this is really delicious!" Suzee said. "I'd love to eat lunch like this every day, but there's no way I could manage it."

"Most of us couldn't. But that's okay—doing it just once a week makes it more extraordinary. We appreciate it more."

The audience murmured their agreement.

After wiping his lips with a napkin, Landry put on a slightly stern expression. "Now, there are a few other things to remember. Don't transport your lunch in those grungy old plastic containers that have been floating around your kitchen since the nineties. Dress that up too. For instance, if you look around a Japanese store or online, you can find some bento boxes that are both darling and practical."

He pictured thousands of women logging into Amazon at that very moment and typing *bento box* into the search bar. He ought to get a kickback.

"During your special lunch," he continued, "keep your phone tucked away, and for goodness' sake, don't do any work! Don't even think about work. This is *you* time."

Suzee looked serious. "So many of us forget to give ourselves that gift."

Landry ignored a twinge of guilt. He could work on his feelings of hypocrisy when he was away from the cameras. "Exactly. But just because it's you time doesn't mean you can't share it. If you have a good friend at work, invite her to join you. You can take turns bringing the food. Or... maybe you can even sneak away somewhere private and have a special someone come to lunch."

The audience oohed and aahed as if eating lunch with their spouses had never occurred to them. Maybe it hadn't. Really, most women in the viewing audience either grabbed a quick sandwich at the office or ate the toddler's leftovers from a plastic Thomas the Train plate while standing over the sink. Which was why they deserved one good lunch per week.

"I like *that* idea a lot," Suzee said.

"When my late husband and I first started getting serious," Landry said, "I used to bring him a nice lunch. We loved that time together."

That was an exaggeration. Yes, a few times early on Landry had showed up at the office and begged Steve to grab a bite with him. But Steve was always too busy with his depositions and briefs and trials, and he'd give Landry a quick kiss before sending him away to eat by himself. Still, Landry had *imagined* elaborate midday meals with Steve—perhaps followed with a little afternoon delight— and it was the thought that counted.

Suzee had known Steve and was aware Landry was stretching the truth. But she nodded anyway. "What lovely memories. I'm so glad you've shared them with us."

The audience clapped enthusiastically. Sometimes Landry felt guilty about trotting out Steve's ghost to boost fan empathy, but Steve wouldn't have minded. When he was alive, he thought Landry was a little silly for mentioning him publicly—"What do I have to do with home décor and the latest clothing styles, Lan?"—but he'd humored Landry in this. Besides, more than one person had written Landry to say she used to oppose same-sex marriage, but hearing about Landry and Steve had changed her mind. *Now I see how normal it is*, they'd say. And Steve would have approved of that completely.

After a brief pause, Suzee stood, and Landry rose to his feet as well. "You've brought a present for our audience, haven't you?" she said. This was his typical MO, but folks still squirmed in excitement.

"Of course. A good guest always brings a small gift." He lifted a square of fabric from the table and held it up. "Everyone here today will get a pair of these beautiful Azulejos do Porto napkins. They're hand-embroidered in Portugal and inspired by the local tile work, and they'll make an excellent beginning to your special lunchtime table setting." Fortunately the company had been willing to supply them for free in exchange for the plug on the *Suzee Show*.

Predictably, the audience reacted as if they'd just won a Vegas jackpot. Suzee had to wait for the uproar to settle. "Landry, thanks so much for bringing us such wonderful inspiration today!"

He executed a shallow bow. "It's always a pleasure."

"Now, I think I've persuaded you to come back next week, right? What do you have in store for us then?"

"I have some great ideas on how to use bullet journaling to get ready for the holidays."

"But it's only August!"

He clapped a hand to his chest in faux shock. "Only August! Suzee, that leaves us only three months to prepare.

We need to get in gear!" Then he leaned in and kissed her cheek, raised his arm to the audience, and swept offstage with as much theatricality as he could muster.

Time to return home, remove his metaphorical mask, and get back to finding the real Landry Bishop. Whoever that was.

AS the crow flies, the *Suzee Show* studio in Burbank wasn't far from Landry's house in Beverly Hills. Fifteen miles, maybe. But Landry wasn't traveling by crow. He was instead in the passenger seat of his personal assistant's Mercedes, catching up on his texts and emails and listening to her swear.

"Don't you dare try to cut me off, pig-fucker!" Elaine Zhang yelled at a Lexus in the next lane.

"You could just let him in," Landry said mildly.

"Are you kidding? That son of a bitch saw the Lane Closed signs just like the rest of us, but he decided he'd try to sneak by. Well, now he can just sit there and rot." She flipped off the other driver for good measure.

"I told you to take Magnolia instead of the 101. You're at least going to get off on Coldwater Canyon, right?"

"Aren't they doing some road repair there?"

Landry sighed. "Right. God, one of these days I'm going to move someplace where the cars actually get to move down the streets instead of just sitting there. And where I don't have a ridiculous mortgage on a house and an equally ridiculous commute time." *As long as that someplace isn't Peril, Nebraska.*

Elaine honked at a minivan before glancing at Landry. "Are you still considering Palm Desert?"

"That was Stevie's idea, not mine."

"Less traffic."

He snorted. "Modesto has less traffic too, but I'm not about to move there. I'm just going to stay here as long as I can afford it. But I get to bitch about the traffic."

"Fair enough."

They inched forward a few feet. Elaine was humming something under her breath, probably an eighties power ballad, and Landry answered a text from one of his editors about an upcoming magazine column. Then he deleted an email from his sister, Missy, without reading it.

"How did today's show go?" Elaine asked.

"It was okay. The audience liked the concept, I think. Suzee was pleased. She asked me again if I want to do a regular segment."

Elaine waited a moment before prompting him. "Well?"

"I told her no again."

"Nice steady income. Could turn into a chance for your own show."

"Yes, I know." He gazed out his window, but there wasn't much to see. A guard rail, some bushes, the yellow hills beyond. There weren't even any billboards on this stretch of highway. If he were in charge at Caltrans, he'd plant wildflowers along the shoulders, a mix that bloomed all year round. Also, if he were in charge of Caltrans, one of his perks might be a special way to move around the state without sitting in traffic. Did Caltrans have helicopters?

"I picked up your suits from the dry cleaner's," Elaine said. "And I tried to get the stain out of that shirt, but it wouldn't budge."

"Did you use cider vinegar and liquid laundry detergent?"

She rolled her eyes. "Yes, Landry. I used cider vinegar and laundry detergent. But blackberry juice seems to bond pretty permanently to silk. You could pretend it's just part of the pattern."

"No, I cannot."

"Then throw it away."

"It's Versace," he said with a slight whine.

"Ask them for another one. They'll give you one if you promise to pimp it."

"It was from last year's collection."

"Then it's old news anyway," she said, shrugging. "Anyway, like I said, I picked up your stuff at the cleaner's. And I packed your suitcase. You wanted to wear the gray cashmere sport coat tomorrow, right? With the black slacks and black turtleneck?"

He thought for a moment. "That's right."

"Sort of a subdued look for you, isn't it?"

"You packed the scarlet hanky, right? That'll make the whole thing pop. Anyway, it's a night show. Something a little more understated is called for." He often dressed in bright colors, but this time he didn't want to march across people's TV screens looking like a parrot. He could pull off elegant as well as electrifying.

They'd reached the Coldwater Canyon exit, but Elaine ignored Landry's wild gesticulations and continued on the freeway. "Van Nuys will be slower yet, even without construction," Landry protested, although it was too late.

"Bummer. But back to the matter at hand. You have the ten-fifteen red-eye out of LAX tonight. I'll come get you at seven so you don't have a stress fit about missing your plane. A driver will pick you up on the other end. Do you want to go to your hotel first or just catch some breakfast before your morning meeting?"

He had to think about that one. "If I go to the hotel, do I have time for a shower?"

"Yeah, but only if you zoom through your hair routine and skimp on the skin care. You'll have time to mess with your hair before the show tapes anyway."

"Fine. Then hotel, no breakfast."

She gave him a quick, stern look. "You'll eat something at the hotel? Wait, don't even bother lying to me. I'll have something delivered to your room."

"Fine," he repeated petulantly, although he secretly liked it when she fussed a little.

"Good. So that's everything for tomorrow. It's New York—you can figure out your own dinner. Your Friday meetings are calendared, your driver's all arranged, and you're booked on the 4:30 p.m. back to LAX. I'll meet you there."

"Thank you," he said. He was very good at showing up when and where he was supposed to—and he'd look damned fine when he arrived—but arranging all the details himself would have spiraled him into anxiety.

"All in a day's work. Which reminds me—" She stomped on the brake to avoid colliding with an old lady in a Buick. "Douchebag! Don't get on the highway if you don't know how to drive!"

While Elaine cursed the lady's offspring and ancestors, Landry steeled himself for what he knew was coming. Elaine had introduced this conversation several times already, and so far he'd been able to shut her down. But she was more stubborn than he was, and eventually she'd win. Now that he was a captive audience, she had him pinned down—unless he was willing to jump out of the Benz and run screaming up the 101.

He seriously considered it.

"Two weeks," Elaine said ominously. "That's all you have left with me."

"Sixteen days," he corrected her.

"During two of which you'll be in New York. Landry, you haven't made any steps toward replacing me."

"You're irreplaceable."

She wasn't sidetracked by his charm. "You need a new personal assistant."

"I don't. I already have the world's most perfect PA."

"Yes, you do. But she's about to quit so she can spend quality time with her family in Hawaii."

"I could move to Hawaii," Landry mumbled.

"Sure, but that puts you pretty far away from your guest appearances and meetings and the rest of your work. Besides, you'd be on your own there too. I'm going to take care of my parents while they're still around, remember?"

Of course he remembered. And he was more than aware of how incredibly selfish he was being. Elaine had worked hard for years, and she deserved to spend time relaxing in tropical comfort. She certainly had the right to choose her relatives over him. And by doting over her aging parents instead of finding some handsome guy and living it up, she'd probably achieve sainthood.

But Elaine had been running his life for a long time, and when she left, Landry would be alone.

"I'm never going to find anyone as good as you," he said.

She grinned. "Nope, probably not, because I'm a goddamn goddess. But you can still find somebody good. What about that guy I sent you last week?"

"He kept saying *hella*. 'Man, your house is hella nice. Wow, you have a hella great view.' I'd end up smacking him within a day and then he'd sue. And I'd be without a PA."

Elaine snorted. "And that sweet girl before him? She has an MA from Tufts and she doesn't say *hella*. She speaks better English than you do."

"Yes, but she wears cheap perfume, which makes me sneeze. And with the fancy graduate degree, how long do you think she'll be happy dealing with my laundry and taxiing me around town?"

"What about the other woman I sent? She doesn't have an MA."

Landry flapped a hand dismissively. "She wants to be an *actress*." That was really all he needed to say.

They'd finally reached the exit, although Elaine had to squeeze the car onto the shoulder to avoid waiting even longer in traffic. Things were moving a bit more briskly on the surface streets. Hoping Elaine had given up, Landry bent over his phone.

But she came to a stoplight and poked him in the knee. "You need a PA. You can't function without one."

"I am a grown man in my late twenties—"

"Thirty-four."

"—in my early thirties, and I can do fine without a PA."

"Uh-huh. Sure." She gunned the engine when the light turned green, then turned a few blocks later onto Beverly Glen, where they began to scale the Hollywood Hills. Almost home, and they were moving faster here. He'd have time for a quick workout and shower, and maybe a light bite to eat before Elaine returned to take him to the airport. He might even have a bit of time to work on that piece he owed the Huffington Post, a take on the upcoming Emmys. Or maybe he'd just deal with that on the plane.

"I'm going to send you another applicant," Elaine said, dashing his hopes.

"But—"

"This kid is different. No graduate degrees, and he has no interest in acting. Actually, he's from Seattle and doesn't know the industry at all."

"Seattle?" Landry sounded as incredulous as if Elaine had told him the guy came from the moon. "So what qualifies him to be my PA?"

She paused. "Nothing, exactly. But he's a nice kid, and I hear he works hard." She sighed. "And he's my sister's husband's brother's son, so he's family."

Landry tried to figure out what relation this person was to Elaine. Step-nephew-in-law? No, that wasn't right.

He tucked the phone into his pocket and crossed his arms. "I'm not in the market for a new PA." He said it quite firmly.

Elaine was silent the remainder of the way home. She used the remote to open the gate and then pulled into his driveway, her face set into a frown. "Seven," she finally said.

"I'll be ready."

Landry strode into the house, focused only on his workout.

Chapter Two

NEW York was a success. After bantering playfully with the talk-show host, Landry told an amusing story about a celebrity—he didn't mention the name—who'd inexplicably attempted home hair-dyeing and ended up with green curls. Landry concluded with a short segment on how to choose a lapel style in men's suits. Afterward, the host seemed honestly pleased and promised him a return visit. Landry had mixed feelings about that. On the one hand, national airtime was valuable. But on the other hand, it involved more cameras, more pretending to be the *Fabulous* Landry Bishop.

After the taping, Landry changed into less formal clothes. He texted a couple of friends, and they spent the evening sampling appetizers in a few of Manhattan's

trendiest restaurants. They had drinks too, all of them
getting slightly tipsy, but even though an adorable
waiter gave his phone number, Landry spent the night
alone in his hotel room.

On Friday he had a morning meeting with a
literary agent to discuss plans for a book: styling tips
for professional men on the go. He had released a
similar volume aimed at women a year earlier, briefly
appearing on the *New York Times* Best Sellers list. He
had lunch with an up-and-coming designer a friend had
told him about, and later a meeting with a cosmetics
exec touting a new line of skin care for men. They both
gave him samples; Landry ended up having to buy an
extra suitcase at a shop near his hotel.

During the return flight, he finished the HuffPost
essay and then dozed through most of a Ryan Reynolds
flick. He couldn't remember the last time he'd seen
a movie in an actual theater. He should remedy that.
Maybe if he found a way to work moviegoing into
one of his talk-show visits, he'd have a good excuse to
go. Hmm. *How to Go On a Movie Date and Feel Like
You're the Star.* That was a possibility.

As promised, Elaine met him at the airport and
watched with amusement as he struggled to fit his extra
luggage in her car. "I saw the show last night," she said
as soon as Landry was in the passenger seat. "You were
great."

"Really? I wasn't too…." He searched for the right
term. Smarmy? Stiff-necked? Punctilious? He knew
he often came across that way. "Unapproachable?" he
finally finished.

"You were cute and funny but also informative."

He sighed with relief. Elaine was honest in her
appraisals, which was something he'd valued since the

day they'd met. In fact, it was the main reason he'd hired her.

"And the meetings were a success too?" She knew they were, because he'd kept her updated via texts, but she also knew he liked to talk about it.

"Yes, definitely. Dana says the new book's a go, which means I better start cracking. Oh, and we came up with another idea as well. How to make your bedroom into a luxurious retreat on a budget."

She laughed. "My bedroom's a dumping ground for unfolded laundry and stuff I keep meaning to read someday."

Landry had never seen Elaine's home. He knew she had a nice apartment in WeHo, close enough that she could get to his house quickly, and without his heart-stopping mortgage. He'd seen the outside of her building a couple of times, when she double-parked the car and ran inside to fetch something. But their relationship had never fully crossed from colleagues to friends, at least not enough for her to invite him over for coffee, and he'd never presumed to ask. Now he wondered if he should have.

"Well," he said, trying to keep his mind on cheerier subjects, "maybe you just need better storage options. My concept for this new book is stylish hacks of items from IKEA, Target, and thrift stores."

"I like it! But it's going to keep you busy."

"It is." He was happy about that. Mostly.

When they arrived at his house, Elaine helped him wrestle the suitcases inside. They took them straight to the master bedroom, where the bed was neatly made and fresh flowers adorned the little table near the window. His housecleaning service was responsible for the bed and the generally spotless state of the place, but Elaine must have arranged the flowers. They were pretty, with sunflowers and mums adding bright colors to his mostly white décor.

Elaine stood near the door, hands on her hips. "Do you need help unpacking? 'Cause if not, I have some stuff to take care of at home."

Landry swallowed a pang of regret. He had hoped she'd be up for a light dinner, maybe some takeout Thai. They could talk about his trip and her Hawaii plans. "I'm fine. But hang on—Gaspard gave me a dress for you."

Elaine looked down at her ample figure skeptically. "Designer clothes for me? They don't come in my size."

"Of course they do. Well, Gaspard's do at any rate. That's his focus, actually. Styles that bring out the beauty of men and women who don't have models' bodies." He unzipped the garment bag and pulled out the dress, a cocktail-length number in black and red with slightly retro styling. He held it up. "You're going to look amazing in this."

The glint in her eyes said she liked it. "Very pretty. But where am I going to wear something like that in Hawaii?"

"Anywhere you want to, my dear. A night out at a nice restaurant. A special occasion at home with your family. Or when you're standing on the lanai drinking lilikoi-guava juice for breakfast and you want to feel extra gorgeous."

She took the hanger from him, draping the dress over her arm. "You're good at that, you know?"

"What?"

"Making people feel like they can be glamorous. I think it's why you're so popular." She said it thoughtfully, as if she'd never considered this before.

"Thank you. I do believe everyone deserves to have at least a little sparkle in their lives."

"You deserve that too." She gave his arm a quick squeeze.

After Elaine left, Landry unpacked and thought about what she'd said. By any objective standard, his life had a *lot* of sparkle: an expensive house in an exclusive neighborhood, designer clothes, a pricy car he rarely had to drive, exquisite meals, and a jet-setting life with talk-show appearances and best-selling books. He was a fortunate man who led an enviable existence. And if his personal life was a little sparse, well, he'd been in love once, and he'd spent seven years with a wonderful man who loved him back. That was enviable too.

As if pulled by invisible strings, Landry wandered out of the bedroom and into his study, which housed his only displayed photo of Steve. It was a picture of the two of them, taken during one of their rare vacations. They stood on a damp, windswept beach in Oregon, both of them looking a little ridiculous in raingear. They had their arms around each other's waists, and Steve, sporting a goofy grin, held a hermit crab in his open palm. His hair was a mess.

"Oh, Stevie," Landry said with a sigh.

And that was enough of that.

Landry returned to the bedroom and considered changing into Armani trousers and a plaid Alexander McQueen button-down. But recognizing that nobody would see him, he allowed himself the luxury of sweatpants and a T-shirt instead. He'd go through the emails he'd neglected over the past day or two, have a little workout in his home gym, and then rustle up something to eat. A stir-fry, maybe. Elaine would have made sure the fridge was stocked with fresh veggies.

Sitting cross-legged on the bed, he picked up his tablet and tapped on his email. He got through the first several without any problem, deleting the spam and sending quick replies to his agent, the *Suzee Show* producer, and the cosmetics exec he'd met in New York. But when he discovered another message from Missy, he just couldn't bring himself to open it. At least he didn't delete it this time. He set the tablet aside instead.

He meandered through his house. It was a really nice place, albeit too big for just one person. In fact it had been too big for two, but when they'd bought it, Landry had held hope for children. Steve had been lukewarm on the idea but had wavered just enough that Landry thought he could persuade him.

So yes. Today only one person lived there.

The house had been built by a prominent architect in the sixties and had remained in the hands of the original owners until they passed away. Steve and Landry got a good deal on it and then spent a small fortune bringing it into the twenty-first century. They kept the basic bones of the structure, including the clerestory windows, the exotic wood floor and trim, and the grand—if unnecessary—fireplaces. But Landry had overseen a complete remodel of the bathrooms and kitchen, marrying midcentury modern with some sleek contemporary lines. They'd also replaced one of the pool-house walls with floor-to-ceiling glass panels that could slide wide open, and they'd turned the structure itself into a small art gallery of sorts. They used to invite their friends over for parties where the food and drinks were in the pool house and the guests would spill out onto the patio. Landry hadn't hosted a party in the eighteen months since Steve died.

Standing in the quiet night beside the still water, Landry missed the laughter.

And then, still in his exercise clothes and with his hair unstyled, he grabbed his wallet and keys from the house, marched into the garage, and stared for a moment at his car. The Jag was impractical in several respects, ranging from its unnecessary horsepower to the metallic black paint that showed every speck of dust. He rarely drove it. But Steve had bought them matching cars as a Christmas gift—and died when his was T-boned by an inattentive truck driver—and Landry couldn't bring himself to trade in his own.

Anyway, he reminded himself as he pulled out of the driveway, the seats were really comfortable.

Feeling as guilty over his destination as a man about to rob a bank, Landry drove down to Sherman Oaks. He would have texted Elaine and asked her to run this errand for him, but she was busy. And there was nobody else in the universe he trusted for this.

As soon as he caught sight of the familiar crossed palm trees, Landry regretted his decision to leave the house. This was stupid. Even a little dangerous. But going back empty-handed would be even more stupid. So he turned into the drive-through and rolled up to the speaker.

"Welcome to In-N-Out!" chirped a tinny female voice. "How can we help you today?"

He didn't even have to read the menu board. "A hamburger, animal style. Fries. With a lot of salt and ketchup, please. And a chocolate shake."

She told him the price, and he pulled up to the window. She took his outstretched twenty without paying attention to him. But she got a good look when she handed back the change.

"Oh my God! You're Lan—"

"No, I'm not."

"You are! You're Landry Bishop! Oh my God! My mom and I watch you on the *Suzee Show* all the time.

You know that one you did on the garden-themed baby shower? We totally did that for my sister 'cause she likes flowers and she, like, absolutely loved it."

Landry smiled wanly at her. "I'm glad to hear that."

"My sister loves you too. She did her baby's room using your ideas, and my mom does your fifteen-minute express workout. Oh! Oh! I totally organized our linen closet just like you said, with all the towels folded right and everything. Will you autograph something? My mom and sister will be so hype!"

"Sure." He took the napkin she gave him, found a pen in his glove box, and looked up at her. "What's your name?"

"Trinity. Oh my God!"

He used the center of the steering wheel as a makeshift desk and carefully wrote a short note: *Dear Trinity, Thank you to you and your family for such enthusiastic support. Yours, Landry Bishop.*

She squealed when he gave it back to her.

By then, several other employees were clustered behind her and peering out at him. "I think there are cars waiting behind me," Landry prompted.

"Oh, yeah, right. Hang on." Trinity disappeared for a moment, then returned to give him his milkshake. She paused with his bag of food in her hand. "Hey, um, not to be like, totally nosy or anything. But aren't you always talking about eating healthy and stuff?" She raised her eyebrows.

"Yes, I do try to encourage a beneficial diet."

She waved the bag slightly. "This isn't very... beneficial."

Shit. Landry thought quickly. "Well, I also believe that we should periodically treat ourselves to something decadent. When we've been especially good about something." *Or when we're longing for a taste of an ordinary, unglamorous life.*

"Oh, right. Sure." Trinity handed him the bag. "Well, you have a good night, Mr. Bishop. And thanks for the autograph!"

"Thank you." He drove away after a forced smile. But he got only as far as the strip mall in the next block, where he parked between a pair of enormous SUVs. He wolfed down the burger and fries, pausing only long enough for slurps of milkshake. Everything was delicious. Yet when nothing remained but the empty containers, Landry tasted bitter defeat. He put all the trash into the bag, which he placed on the passenger seat. Then he picked up his phone and composed a text.

Fine. Set up an interview with your step-great-nephew-in-law.

Chapter Three

LANDRY watched the security cameras as the car rolled through the open gate and stopped in front of his house. The Benz was more familiar than his own Jag, but the person who emerged from the driver's seat bore little resemblance to Elaine. He was male, for one thing, not especially tall, but taller and thinner than Elaine. And instead of her practical bob of straight black hair, he had light hair—the actual color unclear on the black-and-white monitor—held back in a loose ponytail. He wore a suit, but even with the screen's poor resolution, Landry could tell it didn't sit well on him, and not just because it was inexpensive. Landry suspected this was a man who rarely dressed up. The person—who had to be Jordan Stryker—meandered away from the house toward the edge of the property. He stood for a long moment taking in the view, then straightened his back, turned around, and marched to the front door. Landry shuffled away from the monitor, obscurely embarrassed to have been spying. Jordan rang the bell, and he looked startled when Landry opened the door. "Oh! Mr. Bishop."

Landry raised an eyebrow. "Were you expecting someone else?"

"No, I just didn't realize...." Jordan blinked rapidly and then seemed to get himself under control. A wide smile appeared, complete with deep dimples and attractive lines at the outer corners of his blue eyes. He held out a hand. "Sorry. I'm Jordan Stryker. Obviously. And I'm really glad to meet you. Thank you *so* much for agreeing to interview me. I really, really appreciate it 'cause I know you're super busy and everything and Elaine says you have a lot of stuff going on all the time which is pretty cool actually but probably means you don't have much time for interviews and stuff."

They shook hands briefly at the beginning of Jordan's monologue, and then Landry stood with head cocked, trying to decide whether to be annoyed or amused. More the latter, perhaps. Although Jordan had to be close to Landry's age, he had the air of an eager puppy. The kind who slobbered and shed everywhere and probably chewed up your shoes and peed on the carpet but was too cute to be angry at. And he *was* cute: dark blond hair, slightly triangular face, and those goddamn dimples.

When Jordan paused to breathe, Landry stepped back from the doorway. "Follow me, please."

He'd given considerable thought as to where to conduct the interview. The study would have been the obvious choice, but that somehow felt too intimate. Landry had sat with the previous applicants in his living room, but he'd felt the urge to act as host rather than prospective employer, and that wasn't right. So today he led Jordan through the house and out to the backyard.

"Wow, that's cool how you can open the whole living room up to the outdoors," Jordan commented, patting a sliding glass door as he passed it. "Makes a lot of sense here where the weather's always perfect. Back in Seattle we'd probably only get to open stuff up a few days a year."

Landry answered with a noncommittal hum and took them to one of the patio tables currently shaded by the house. "Please, sit." He gestured before taking his own seat.

It was interesting to watch Jordan arrange himself. He began with a straight back and knees directly in front of him, forearms resting lightly on the table's edge. But he almost immediately began to slump and sprawl. Then he seemed to catch himself and sat upright again with a jerk. "I brought my résumé." He reached for his inner jacket pocket.

"You emailed it to me," Landry reminded him. "I've looked it over quite thoroughly, and I don't need a hard copy." In any case it contained little information pertinent to the position.

Jordan relaxed again. "Right. Well, if you change your mind, let me know. Um, wow. Your house is so beautiful. I mean, of course it is, right? Not like you'd be living in a shack or anything. But this place is special. I bet you put a ton of time into making it so nice."

Jordan's opinion shouldn't have mattered, and as an applicant, of course he might try to ingratiate himself. But his words pleased Landry, who *had* put considerable time and effort into his home.

"You don't have experience as a personal assistant." He injected a bit of sternness into the statement, as if it were an accusation.

"No. I mostly worked in stores and restaurants and stuff when I was younger. More recently I've been an in-home caregiver for the sick and elderly. Which you know from my résumé already. Duh. Sorry."

"So what qualifies you for this position?"

"I like to help people—I really do. Like, make their lives easier. That's what I did with my other jobs. Even when I was a store clerk, I tried to figure out what customers needed and wanted, and I did my best to make them happy. And of course when I care for people, it's my job to make them as comfortable as possible, to do all those little things for them so they can enjoy life as much as possible. Plus I pretty much have no life of my own, which means I can devote myself to my boss 24/7. I might not know all the details of how to do this job, but I'll learn them—fast. The most important thing, Mr. Bishop, is that I know how to take care of people. It's my superpower. And it's what I love." He patted his heart as if to demonstrate his sincerity.

This response surprised Landry, who'd expected something closer to *I'm a hard worker who learns quickly.* Jordan's words felt more sincere than the standard generic assertions. Something about Jordan intrigued Landry, and it wasn't just his handsome face.

Landry sighed and allowed himself to lean back. He didn't want to be influenced by his loyalty to Elaine or the allure of Jordan's good looks. He needed to be a businessman, dammit, rational and perceptive. Ruled by his head, not his heart or his dick. He had no use for his heart and his dick—beyond the biological necessities, of course.

Jordan was taking advantage of Landry's quiet to look around more carefully. Landry watched as his gaze skimmed over the pool, rested for a moment on the view, and then moved to the pool house, where the collection of paintings was visible through the glass wall.

"What's that?" Jordan blurted, pointing at the pool house. He grimaced and dropped his hand. "Sorry. You're the one who's supposed to be asking questions, not me."

"Why don't you tell me what you expect this job to entail?" Hey, that was a clever one. Score a point for the rational brain.

Jordan scratched his upper lip while he considered. "Elaine told me some of what she does. Driving you places, setting appointments, doing errands... things like that. But maybe I could just summarize?"

"All right."

"I think your personal assistant makes sure your life runs smoothly. They concentrate on the details so you can give your energy to your work and the other things you want to do instead of sweating the small stuff. If an assistant is really good, they figure out what you need before you do."

That was an accurate précis. Maybe Elaine had coached him.

Landry laced his hands and set them on the tabletop. "You haven't remained at your previous positions very long."

"I think the longest was, um... two years? Around that. But yeah."

"Why?"

"In a few cases, I quit because the place wasn't run well. Sometimes the management just sucks, right? Like this one restaurant, they used to be great, but they started cutting corners. They were treating the whole staff like crap, which was bad enough, but they also found sneaky ways to screw over the customers." He shrugged. "I got tired of being shortchanged and having to make excuses to people who'd laid out a lot of money for a meal."

Landry knew enough about the food-service and retail industries to find Jordan's story credible, but he raised his eyebrow again. "Were *all* your employers unscrupulous?"

"No, no, some of them were fantastic. But…. Okay. I'm gonna be honest. When I was younger, I used to be flaky. I got fired sometimes for fooling around during slow times at work or being late. And I got bored easily, so I'd want to try something else. I promise I'm more settled now. I've loved my caregiver placements. I'm good at taking care of people, I really am." Jordan sighed. "I don't think I'm very good at job interviews, though. People tell me I don't have a good filter. But I think I could become a truly great PA—I wish I could show you that."

He looked… distressed wasn't the right word. *Tired.* Yes, that was it. As if he'd been making enormous efforts for a long time and was almost too fatigued to go on.

"Why don't you tell me why you want this particular position."

"Well, I want to try something new. I want a fresh challenge that builds on what I already love. I think I'd be good at this. But also… okay, this is gonna sound weird, but I can't think of a better way to put it. I want to make a difference to someone. Long-term." He leaned forward, his eyes sparkling with emotion. Pretty eyes. "It's great to take care of people who, you know, are too sick to do it all themselves. But that doesn't last.

They get better or… or they don't. I want something more. I want to make a real difference in someone's life. Help ease his way so he can fly."

"I'm not a project." Landry's tone was sharp.

"I know. You're a person. And you're super successful and super busy. But I can help smooth over all the bumps. I'd love it if now and then you could realize how well your life is flowing, and you could spend a second or two thinking, *Hey, that Jordan's really worth the bucks I'm paying him.*"

Damn it. Well, at least Jordan hadn't said *hella* even once, and he didn't want to be an actor. And there was something so *bright* about him. A vitality that called to something deep inside Landry's soul.

Landry leaned forward. "Let's discuss the details, shall we?"

SOME of the details were easy. Jordan could start immediately, which meant he'd shadow Elaine for her last few days on the job. He said his parents would ship his belongings down from Seattle. He was perfectly satisfied with the salary and terms of employment Landry offered. And when Landry gave him a thorough tour of the property, explaining how things were supposed to work and what chores he expected to be completed, Jordan asked good questions and took notes on the back of his résumé. He also enthused about the house and furnishings, but not so much as to interfere with the business at hand. And he hung on Landry's every word, even during the explanation of how the garbage collection worked.

Other details proved more complicated. Such as transportation. "What kind of car do you own?" Landry asked as they stood in the kitchen.

"Um... none. But I can save up my salary and get one."

Landry frowned. That wouldn't do at all. He made a mental note to discuss the matter with Elaine. She was planning on selling her Benz before she moved to Hawaii anyway, so maybe he'd buy it from her for Jordan's use.

But another issue overshadowed this one. "Where do you plan to live?" Landry asked.

"Elaine says I can stay with her until she moves. She's letting me crash on her couch."

"Will you take over her apartment after that?"

"Can't. Her lease is up, and they've already rented the place to someone else. For way more money. I'll look around and find something."

Landry scowled more deeply. Although he paid a decent wage, it would be hard for Jordan to find affordable housing nearby. And Landry didn't want him living too far away; he needed his PA available on short notice.

Jordan twitched his shoulders. "I, um, could rent a room from you maybe. 'Cause you have extras. Then I'd be right here anytime you need me. I promise I'm totally quiet, and neat too. I've been living with either my parents or some of my caregiver clients, so, you know, I'm used to house rules." He smiled winningly.

On the one hand, Jordan was correct. The house held plenty of room for another person, and Landry having his PA at hand could be very convenient. But Jordan was a complete stranger, and Landry wasn't used to sharing with anyone but Steve. Besides, Jordan's mere presence

made Landry's heart beat a little faster than usual, and
his cheeks felt ready to flush at a moment's notice. The
man was… compelling. Which Landry didn't need in an
employee.

"I won't cramp your style," Jordan said, misconstruing
Landry's silence. "I'll totally stay out of the way when
you have guests over, unless you want me to help with
something. And if you have a date over, I'll make myself
scarce. You won't even know I'm here."

"I don't have dates over." He didn't have dates,
period. He'd gone out with a couple of guys after Steve
died, but none of them stuck. They'd been nice enough,
but he hadn't felt an emotional connection. Yes, he became
sexually frustrated at times, but he could take care of that
solo. Hell, he could write a book on how to take care of it
solo. Maybe he should suggest that to Dana instead of the
IKEA hacks. Landry Bishop, Master of Masturbation.

And that was not where his mind needed to be
right now.

"Pool house," he said, startling himself and confusing
Jordan.

"Excuse me?"

"You can stay in the pool house. It has a full bath,
and it's larger than any of the secondary bedrooms.
There are curtains on the glass wall to give you privacy.
We'd have to move out the paintings and move in some
suitable furniture, but it would work well."

It made perfect sense. Pool-house residents were
common in Los Angeles, and it wasn't as if Landry
were truly using the space anymore.

But Jordan's pretty mouth turned down slightly.

"You don't care for the idea?" asked Landry.

"No! I mean, yes! I mean—shit. Sorry. It's a great
idea. I love it. Except I like the paintings. So it'd be

kinda cool if they stayed. Otherwise the walls are gonna be blank. Um, unless you have somewhere else you want to hang them."

Landry didn't. There wasn't a truly suitable space in the house—not unless he undertook a major redecorating project—and he didn't want to put them into storage. He'd chosen those paintings himself. And if he was pleased that Jordan liked them too, well, that was irrelevant.

"They can stay. But you must be careful with them."

"Cool! And of course. Really, I know my early work history was a little messy, but I'm not. I know how to take care of things." He moved a step closer to Landry—near enough to touch—and his eyes shone with earnestness. "And how to take care of people too."

If Jordan's smile held promises, Landry decided to sidestep them. He just needed someone to pick up his dry cleaning.

Chapter Four

"YOU are a clever man, Landry."

Elaine missed the eye roll he made in response, since her gaze was fixed on the burly men frolicking in the pool.

"It's hot," Landry said. Which was true—a heat wave had raised temps to near 100.

"Uh-huh."

"Moving furniture is hard work. They were sweaty."

"Yes, yes, they were. And you are a humanitarian."

Landry might have responded with something witty, but then one of the men climbed out of the water—his tighty-whities now completely transparent—directed a wave at Landry and Elaine, and then dove back in. Landry simply sighed.

They both stood there, staring, until bare feet padded on the concrete behind them. Landry turned to see Jordan approaching with a tray of frosted glasses and a large pitcher. "I still say beer's better than iced tea," Jordan announced as he placed the tray on a table.

"And something with citrus and tequila or rum might be best of all. But these gentlemen have to return to work eventually and therefore need to stay sober."

"Yeah, I guess. But you don't. Want me to get you something boozy?"

Although Landry was tempted, he shook his head. "Not now, thank you. I have work to accomplish today too. But you can help yourself if you like. You're off duty for the afternoon, so you can get your room settled."

Jordan glanced at Elaine—already clutching a glass of her famous homemade sangria—then squared his shoulders and looked back at Landry. "I don't do alcohol. I had some issues with it before. Nothing… I never hit rock bottom or anything, but I'm better off avoiding it. I should have told you before. I'm sorry."

"If it's not going to interfere with your job, it's none of my business." Landry was glad to see Jordan brighten at his response, and added, "Your new health benefits include counseling, so if you feel you need some help, you can get it."

Jordan's wide smile appeared. "Thanks. I'm cool. It's been a long time since I touched the stuff."

Landry nodded briskly. "All right. Perhaps you could offer those gentlemen some tea?"

As Jordan trotted to the pool, Elaine fixed Landry with a look. "You sound like an eighty-year-old member of the House of Lords when you say that."

"Say what?"

"Offer those gentlemen some tea," she echoed in a horrible British accent. "Cheerio and pip-pip."

"I don't sound like that."

"Okay, maybe not exactly. But you're totally channeling Lord Thistlebottom." She took a healthy sip of her sangria.

Landry had no good response, in part because he knew she was right—he *did* sound stuffy. But speaking properly was hardly a cardinal sin, was it?

Elaine stepped closer and dropped her voice. "He's going to work out okay for you." She waved her glass toward Jordan, crouched in conversation with the men in the pool. "It really has been a long time since he drank."

"I'm quite willing to take his word on that."

"I'm glad. He's a good kid, he really is. It just took him a while to grow up."

It was funny she put it like that, because Landry had just been thinking how youthful Jordan looked as he laughed beside the water. Jordan was only two years younger than him, yet Landry felt as if they belonged to different generations. Maybe it was the fault of Lord Thistlebottom's ghost.

Jordan returned, followed by a retinue of wet, muscular, nearly naked men, and Landry's thoughts fled. Jordan poured glasses of iced tea, and the furniture movers converged around Landry in a glistening, bulging crowd. "Thanks so much for the break, Mr. Bishop," said a man with sepia skin and large gold nipple rings. "This really hits the spot."

"It must be miserable moving furniture in such weather. I'm glad I could help."

Another man—with a ginger beard and pale, freckled skin that threatened to erupt into sunburn at any moment—sidled a bit closer. "Usually we're lucky if someone offers us water."

The proximity of so much damp masculinity was almost too much for Landry, who was in the midst of a very long sexual dry spell. His face felt flushed. He wished he'd taken up Jordan's offer of something alcoholic. "Well, I appreciate your hard work," he said and then winced at the unintended double entendre.

Nipple-rings didn't wince. He waggled his eyebrows. "I like to work hard. And play hard."

Landry made a slightly strangled noise, at which point Elaine tapped his shoulder. "It's time for that phone call with Ms. Winfrey."

He didn't have any calls scheduled—with Oprah or otherwise—but he gave a quick nod. "Of course. Gentlemen." He nodded at the movers before walking to the house with as much dignity as he could manage.

Half an hour later, while Landry was puttering around with an experimental tabbouleh recipe, Jordan and Elaine joined him in the kitchen. "Try this," he ordered, handing them each a spoonful.

Jordan made approving noises, but Elaine frowned. "That's not a grain."

"It's cauliflower."

"For the love of God, why?"

"For people who want to eat grain-free."

"If you don't want to eat grains, you shouldn't be eating tabbouleh." She took Jordan's spoon along with her own and washed them in the sink.

"I like it," Jordan announced. "It's kind of crunchyish." He seemed sincere.

"Thank you," Landry said.

"Hey, um, you didn't really have an important phone call, did you?"

"No. That was Elaine rescuing me."

"I kinda figured. Except... I hope this doesn't sound rude, but why did you need rescuing? Those guys were *hot*. That whole thing was like the opening of a pretty good porno, you know? If they'd been all over *me* like that, I sure as hell wouldn't have wanted rescuing."

Landry pushed aside the interesting information that Jordan was attracted to men. His PA's sexual orientation was irrelevant. He also pushed aside a stupid and inexplicable jab of jealousy. If Jordan wanted to fantasize about group sex with hunky furniture deliverymen, that was none of Landry's business. So he focused on the question itself.

"Why do you think those extremely attractive men were so interested in me?"

"Um, because they were throwing themselves all over you."

"Yes, I suppose they were. But why? Why *me*?"

"'Cause you're damned hot too."

Even as Landry's face heated at the unexpected compliment, Jordan's cheeks turned a charming shade of pink. Interesting. Their gazes locked so tightly that Landry wondered if either of them would ever look away. Or if he wanted them to.

Then Elaine mumbled, "Oh, for fuck's sake," and whacked Jordan on the shoulder. "What your new boss means, kid, is that although, yes, he *is* obnoxiously good-looking, pretty is a dime a dozen around here. They were panting over him because he's the fabulous, famous Landry Bishop, and they're all wannabe actors looking to break into showbiz."

Landry nodded his agreement, although he could have argued about the good-looking part. He was average. Oh, he knew how to use clothing, hairstyle, and posture to his advantage, but that was just a facade, like wrapping an ordinary gift in expensive glittery paper.

"How do you know they want to be actors?" Confusion wrinkled Jordan's brow.

Elaine and Landry laughed in unison. "We're in LA, honey," she said. "Everyone wants that."

"I don't."

The sweet and plaintive quality of Jordan's reply almost thawed Landry's cynical heart. He wanted to pat Jordan on the back and tell him he was fine just as he was, that it was hardly a character flaw if someone lacked ambition regarding the industry. In fact, the lack of that particular ambition in this town made someone unique. Special.

"Did you get all of your belongings put away already?" Landry asked, moving away from them and toward the fridge. The tabbouleh would suffice. Now he needed to work on the menu for a preholiday tea party he intended to showcase on the *Suzee Show*. He'd need to choose items that were festive but light and that didn't echo traditional holiday meals. And he needed to think about anything other than his new PA.

"Yep," answered Jordan as Landry assessed the contents of the refrigerator. "And you ordered really nice furniture. I like it."

Knowing Jordan wouldn't see, Landry allowed himself a pleased smile. "It's more contemporary than my usual style, but better suited to the pool house, I think." And better suited to Jordan as well.

"It's great. Do you think maybe sometime you could teach me how to pick out decent stuff? Um, if you're not too busy. You're probably too busy."

Landry turned his head to look at Jordan. "I'm sure we can find some time to at least go over the basics."

"Great! Thanks! And is there anything you want me to do now?"

"Take the afternoon off. Settle in, get comfortable. Use the pool if you want."

"He'll start exploiting your labor tomorrow," Elaine said.

Ignoring her, Landry closed the refrigerator doors and faced Jordan. "We'll meet tomorrow at eight after my morning exercise and go over the week's schedule and my expectations for you."

Jordan grinned. "I'm looking forward to being exploited."

Landry leaned against a counter and watched Jordan lope across the patio to the pool house. He didn't realize he'd sighed until Elaine came up beside him. "Wow," she said.

"What?"

"You two."

"What about us?"

"I'm sorta regretting I'll be in Hawaii. Gonna miss the fireworks."

"What fireworks?"

She simply smiled and shook her head.

ALTHOUGH Landry haunted his study that evening, he got very little accomplished. He attempted to work on the outline of one of his new books. When that got him nowhere, he tried clicking through Pinterest in hopes of inspiration for clever Christmas decorations children could make with some adult help. He also envisioned a *Suzee Show* segment on keeping young Thanksgiving guests occupied with holiday craft projects, but mason jar snowmen, greeting card display boards, and candy cane candle holders didn't spark his interest. He found his gaze repeatedly straying to the door.

Having another person in his home was unsettling in a way he couldn't define. Elaine spent a lot of time at his place, frequently at odd hours, but this wasn't the same. Knowing that Jordan was so close at hand, maybe sitting on the furniture Landry had chosen just for him, did obnoxiously fluttery things to Landry's thoughts. And while he might camp things up onstage at times, Landry wasn't a fluttery man. He prided himself on practicality, in fact, but his current feelings toward Jordan weren't at all practical.

He shouldn't be letting his mind wander to thoughts of Jordan. To images of him settling into the pool house, tucking his clothing into the closet and dresser, arranging the pillows just right on the bed. To Jordan's broad-fingered hands and speculations about how they'd feel skating across Landry's heated skin. To flashes of Jordan kneeling naked on a throw rug, his lips quirked in a delighted smile, his fingers fumbling at Landry's trouser button. Because those last thoughts, they weren't just impractical, they were damning. And Landry had no intention of ending up embroiled in a lawsuit and losing his new PA.

Finally, out of near desperation, Landry opened his email account and, having taken care of the more recent communications, found Missy's name at the top of the list. Although it pained him to do so, he clicked the message open.

Hi Wormy,

"Ugh." The hated childhood nickname was too much for him, and he closed the window. He'd specifically asked her *not* to call him that, more than once, and she always ignored him. He was almost tempted to use her nickname, dating from when she'd become so engrossed in first-grade story time that she wet her pants. "Pissy Missy," he grumbled to himself. That made him feel better, but not enough to face whatever she had to say.

Maybe some nice cucumber water would clear his head.

He marched purposefully into the kitchen, where he pulled a glass out of the cupboard. But as he walked toward the fridge, he glanced outside and froze in place.

Jordan sat on the edge of the pool with his legs dangling in the water. He wore a black T-shirt and khaki shorts—nothing especially revealing or sexy. But he'd tipped his head back, and the pool lights played over his upraised face, giving him an otherworldly aspect. It was as if a gifted sculptor had created the perfect decoration for Landry's patio. Except, of course, Jordan was no mere artwork; he was a living, breathing human being.

Landry fetched a second glass and filled them both from the pitcher in the fridge. Then he crossed the room, opened a door, and padded barefoot across the patio.

"Do you need something?" Jordan shifted as if ready to stand.

Landry waved at him to stay put. "No. Here. Have a drink." He held out the glass.

"Nonalcoholic?"

"Cucumber water."

For some reason that made Jordan laugh. But he took the glass and had a sip, and for a moment they both watched the pool water ripple, Landry standing and Jordan sitting. Jordan's body language was relaxed and easy, with no hints of the tiredness he'd shown during his interview. He looked like a man who'd found contentment. Landry envied him.

"I don't know a single person in Seattle who has their own pool," Jordan finally said.

"I wouldn't imagine they'd be useful in that climate."

"Not really, no. But they're pretty cool here. You really don't mind if I use yours when I'm off duty?"

"Of course not."

"Thanks."

"What made you decide to leave Seattle?" The question had been niggling at Landry for some time, but he hadn't felt comfortable enough to ask it. Posing the question was easier here in the dark, with a cricket chirping softly from the bushes.

"I love Seattle—it's a fantastic city. But I think I was sort of going in circles there. I guess sometimes if you want to get somewhere with your life, you need to physically move away."

Landry nodded in agreement.

A jet flashed overhead, perhaps on its way out of John Wayne Airport, and the warm breeze played with Jordan's fair hair. Landry decided that next time he'd make strawberry or melon water instead. Something a tad sweeter.

"I really appreciate you giving me a chance," said Jordan. "I'm going to try hard to make you glad you did."

"I can be demanding."

"Yeah, that's what Elaine says. But I don't mind a challenge. And anyway, she tells me you're a good guy, so I can handle it."

Inordinately pleased by the secondhand compliment, Landry made a humming noise and drank more water. A part of him—buried deep—had always wondered if Elaine really liked him or whether she simply tolerated him for the paycheck.

"Um, the drinking thing," Jordan began.

"I told you. It's fine."

"Yeah, I know. And I appreciate that too."

"This is Hollywood. A lot of people have problems with drugs or alcohol."

"I bet they do, but you're not hiring them. Or letting them stay at your house. So… thanks." He looked and sounded so earnest that Landry wanted to warn him that naked emotion got you nowhere. *You must build high walls. You must create a facade.*

While Landry took another sip of water, Jordan swung his legs slowly, creating little eddies and splashes. The movement was hypnotizing—so much so that Landry found himself setting his glass on the patio, rolling up the cuffs of his trousers, and sitting beside Jordan on the edge of the pool. The water felt good. When was the last time he'd used the pool for anything but hard exercise? Maybe in the spring he'd do a piece on creative pool parties. Something beyond the boring beer and barbecue. He gazed up at the sky as if he might find inspiration there.

"I miss the stars," he heard himself say.

"I bet you meet a lot of celebrities."

Landry chuckled. "Not that kind of stars. Those." He pointed up.

"What do you mean? There are a bunch of stars up there."

"You only think that because you're used to Seattle. When I was a boy, I could lie back in a field and see the entire Milky Way swirling above me." He'd even learned many of the constellations, although he'd long since forgotten most of them. There hadn't been much point in remembering.

"Where was that field?" Jordan asked softly, as if the answer mattered to him.

"Just outside of Peril, Nebraska."

"Sorry. I've never heard of it."

"There's no reason you should have. It's a small town in the middle of nowhere. But the air was clear and there was almost no light pollution, so it was a good place for stargazing." Huh. That might have been the nicest thing he'd ever said about his hometown.

"So you know what I mean about needing to move away in order to find yourself. Do you go back and visit?"

"No," Landry replied, laughing at the notion. "Why would I? The stars aren't a big enough draw."

"Family?"

Landry shrugged. He'd offered to fly some of them to California for a visit, but they'd claimed to be busy with work and kids. He'd always suspected it was a form of denial, that on some level they knew that if they spent time in LA, Peril would permanently pale in comparison. And that was fine. They seemed content enough with their sweltering summers and frigid winters, their lack of dining and entertainment options, their monotonous scenery. And their endless numbers of stars.

He stood and retrieved his glass. "I have work to do, and tomorrow's a busy day."

"Do you need anything from me tonight?"

Nothing I dare ask of you. "No."

"Do you mind if I hang out in the pool for a while?"

"No."

"I was thinking about actually swimming."

"Go ahead."

Jordan looked up at him with a grin. "I don't own a bathing suit. Is underwear okay? It worked for those furniture guys today."

Landry's cheeks heated—not at the memory of the movers in wet underwear but at the mental image of Jordan wearing almost nothing. He cleared his throat. "There's no rule against it."

"Cool. I'll get some trunks soon. You don't want to join me? Water feels great."

"I have work to do," Landry repeated. As he marched back into the house, he sensed Jordan watching him.

Chapter Five

ELAINE stood in the driveway and stared at the piece of paper in her hands. "You're not serious."

"I wouldn't tease you like that."

"But that's… that's a fucking lot of zeroes, Landry."

"You've earned them."

He'd given a lot of thought to how to end his professional relationship with Elaine. Not with a farewell party; she'd had one of those with her friends. And although she'd invited him, he declined. It would have been awkward, and he didn't want that to ruin her event. She didn't need any tangible gifts, not when she was having to ship her belongings to Hawaii. Cash, however, was portable and always useful, and he could certainly spare some of that.

"You've always paid me plenty well," she said. Tears coursed down her face, but she ignored them.

"This isn't a salary. It's a token of my appreciation and an effort to help you settle happily into your new life."

"Fifty grand is gonna bring a whole lot of happy, all right." She tucked the check back into the envelope and tossed it onto the driver's seat of the Benz. Then she threw herself at Landry and, before he could defend himself, flung her arms around him in a powerful embrace.

His own eyes were a bit leaky too.

She eventually pulled away, but only far enough to whisper into his ear. "You're not my boss anymore, so I'm gonna tell it to you straight."

"You've always told it to me straight. It's one of the things I've valued about you."

"Oh no, kiddo. I've held back. Not anymore, though. So hear me out."

If she weren't still clutching his shoulders, he might have run away. Instead he took a deep, steadying breath. "Yes?"

"You are a really great human being. Not because you know how to dress or because you can decorate the hell out of a house. And not because you have a lot of dough and show up on TV. You're kind and sweet and generous, and you truly want to help improve other people's lives."

"Elaine—"

"Shut it. I'm talking. You need to take some time to improve your own life too, kiddo. Find some friends who appreciate you. Get a boyfriend who cares about the real Landry, not that famous guy. Open up and be your real self. Be happy."

He tried to answer, but she kissed him on both cheeks. Sloppy kisses, the kind that left lipstick marks behind. "Be more of who you want to be instead of who you think you should be," she said. One more kiss after that, and then she detached herself and got into the car, moving the envelope out of the way at the last second. She shoved it in her purse and rifled around for something, perhaps a tissue to wipe away her tears.

Jordan had been waiting in the passenger seat the entire time, and although he'd pretended to be focused on his phone, Landry knew better. He wondered what Jordan had made of the scene, and whether he'd heard what Elaine had said. Not that it mattered. She was just being emotional, was all.

Landry watched them drive away; Elaine waved at him from the bottom of the driveway before the gate closed. "I *am* who I want to be," he muttered as he walked back into the house. Hell, he'd dreamed of this life for years. When he was a kid, instead of skulking in the library with anatomy books or explicit romances, like some of his classmates, he'd snuck looks at lifestyle magazines. *Vogue. House Beautiful. Gourmet.* He watched talk shows that included celebrity guests, taking careful note of what they wore and how they spoke. He sighed over photographs of mansions in Malibu and Beverly Hills.

And now here he was with his own mansion, and he was the one invited for interviews on TV. He got fan mail. People recognized him on the street and begged for autographs and selfies. His bank accounts were comfortably full. He was somebody.

Of course this was the somebody he wanted to be.

LANDRY looked up from his desk when a light knock sounded on the study door.

"Sorry," Jordan said. "Didn't want to interrupt, but I thought you might want me to be doing something."

"Elaine made her flight all right?"

"Yep. And she gave me about a zillion instructions while we were driving there. I took notes. So now I know what kind of groceries you like stocked and where I should take your dry cleaning and how often you need a dentist appointment. In case you need me to do any of that."

"Not right now," Landry said, "although you could make a shopping trip later. Have you checked my calendar?"

"You have a lunch meeting at one with MacKenzye, another meeting in Burbank at four, and a reception tonight at eight."

"Please set out appropriate outfits for each. We'll leave for lunch in an hour."

"Got it." Jordan trotted off.

This was a test, and probably a hard one. Landry owned a lot of clothing and had particular tastes about what should be worn for which occasion. He hadn't lectured Jordan on this subject yet. In fact, Landry hadn't often expected Elaine to do this particular task, although she packed for his trips.

After fifteen minutes had passed, Landry went to his bedroom, where he discovered three outfits spread atop the bed as if a trio of well-dressed men had paid a visit and then suddenly dematerialized. One of the ensembles consisted of a pair of jeans, a white button-down, and a turquoise cashmere sweater. It wouldn't do for any of his engagements. But the other outfits were variations on a theme—suit and silk shirt—and they'd be fine.

"Are these okay?" Jordan asked from the doorway. He appeared slightly nervous.

"The suits are fine, if a bit on the conservative side."

"Not the sweater?"

"Too casual."

"Oh." Jordan scrunched up his face. "I thought, well, SoCal, so maybe too much formality was a no-go. Plus that color totally goes with your eyes."

That made Landry blink. Yes, his eyes were an odd shifting blue-green mix, but he hadn't expected Jordan to notice that detail. "I'd wear it for a weekend outing."

"No comfy jeans and old tee for you, huh?" Jordan looked down at his own clothing, which was exactly that: worn denim and a T-shirt bearing a faded image of what might be Bigfoot. It looked comfortable and suited Jordan fine when not in public, but Landry would look ridiculous dressed like that in front of other people.

"No," Landry said.

"Okay. Let me give this another shot." After getting Landry's nod of approval, Jordan trotted into the walk-in closet. Landry followed but waited in the doorway, watching.

Ignoring the area of the closet with Landry's suits, Jordan zeroed in on the shirts, sliding each hanger to one side so he could consider its contents. Three or four times he lifted a hanger off the pole entirely and held the shirt in midair. He glanced back and forth between it and Landry before returning the hanger to its place. A slight line of concentration showed between his brows, and he nibbled thoughtfully at his lower lip—neither of which should have made Landry slightly giddy, but they did. Even more disconcerting, though, was the way Jordan *looked* at him. As if Landry were a puzzle he truly wanted to solve.

Finally Jordan nodded. "This one." He'd chosen a slim-fitting dress shirt with a tiny red-and-blue floral print.

"Why that one?"

"It's bright and interesting. Like you. I bet you look amazing in it. And the cotton is really soft, so you'll be comfortable wearing it. How much does a shirt like this cost anyway?"

Landry had to think for a moment. "Four or five hundred dollars." That sounded ridiculous when he said it out loud. As if he were bragging.

But Jordan simply grinned. "Wow. Well, you'll look like a million bucks in it. Now let me find you some pants."

By the time they left for Landry's first meeting, Jordan had changed clothes too. He wore khakis, a dress shirt, and a tie, all of which he might have purchased at Old Navy or Target. Landry would have to take him shopping soon. It wasn't that Jordan looked bad, and he didn't need five-hundred-dollar shirts, but Landry Bishop's PA shouldn't resemble a college student on his first day of an internship.

Although the Benz was familiar, the ride to lunch wasn't, mostly because Jordan drove very differently than Elaine. More hesitant, with less swearing, and faithfully following his phone's navigational directions instead of forging his own route. Also, he was male and handsome and smelled of something slightly spicy—deodorant or aftershave perhaps—and he chatted nonstop. He commented on the other drivers, on the homes and businesses they passed, and on how much he loved the Benz. Landry didn't mind the talking, although he rarely responded. Jordan didn't seem to expect him to.

The restaurant, which was in Hollywood, had not been Landry's choice. It was new and very trendy, with a lovely dining room and a pretentious French-Vietnamese menu that promised far more than it accomplished. MacKenzye, a beautiful and somewhat talented singer, had chosen the place more for the exposure than the cuisine. It was the sort of place where someone at the top of the *Billboard* charts was supposed to eat lunch.

"Do you want me to park nearby?" Jordan asked as he pulled to a stop in front of the restaurant.

"If you can find a spot. If not, you can go home. We'll be done here in an hour. Make sure you eat something too."

Jordan's smile was sunny. "Cool. I saw a taco place a couple of miles back."

Suppressing a twinge of jealousy—Landry hadn't had tacos in years—he got out of the car. "One hour," he said briskly.

Despite the mediocrity of the cuisine, lunch went well. MacKenzye wanted to launch a line of cosmetics and moderately priced jewelry, and she sought Landry's advice on how to begin and what to avoid. He'd coached other celebrities on similar topics. Some of them listened and some didn't, but they all paid handsomely for the service. MacKenzye seemed like one who'd heed his advice.

Jordan picked him up promptly, but with a spot of salsa on his shirt. Now he smelled of fried corn and spicy meat. Landry caught himself licking his lips.

"Did your meeting go well?" Jordan asked as he pulled into traffic.

"Yes."

"Cool. Those tacos were *boss*. Not fancy like whatever you ate, though. I bet you didn't have paper napkins and a self-service Coke machine."

"No, I didn't." Landry could picture the taco place—sticky floors, plastic tabletops, a long counter where customers could fill small containers with pico de gallo, salsa roja, salsa verde, slices of lime… maybe even some guacamole and sour cream. The tables would be crowded with blue-collar workers, families with little kids, teenagers joking loudly with each other. Mexican pop music would play over the loudspeakers. There would be no celebrities, and he'd be able to feed an entire family for what MacKenzye had paid for Landry's beautifully composed but bland-tasting banh mi salad.

He became so caught up in the mental image that he ended up less than annoyed at Jordan's slangy use of *boss*. At least it wasn't *hella*, and Jordan's enthusiasm was… sort of cute.

Jordan braked abruptly when a car pulled out in front of him, but he didn't honk. Didn't even call the other driver anything evil. Instead, he was smiling. "I worked at a Mexican place for a while. It was kind of a dump, but it was walking distance from where I lived and I didn't have a car. The best thing, though, was the Salvadoran bakery place next door. I spent three months practically living on guava pastries and leftover tortilla chips."

"It sounds pleasant."

Jordan laughed. "I'd rather work for you any day. Even without the pastries."

Landry almost suggested they stop at a bakery he knew. It was on the way. But he remained silent.

BACK at home, Landry had a short period to answer some emails and change into a suit, and then it was time for his Burbank meeting. This one was with a TV producer who'd seen him on the *Suzee Show* and wanted to discuss the possibility of developing a local Landry show. Landry wasn't interested. But it never hurt to hear a producer out, so he'd accepted the meeting.

Landry spoke to the producer while Jordan— who'd changed into a clean shirt—sat in the reception area. He was supposed to be arranging some future appointments for Landry, but judging from the laughter wafting in through the door, he was socializing with the cute receptionist instead. Landry told himself he was annoyed, not jealous.

"Is there going to be a *Landry Show*?" Jordan asked as they drove back home.

"Unlikely."

"But you're so popular!"

"I don't want my own show."

Jordan paused a few minutes before responding. "How come? I've seen you on TV. You're great."

"I have too much else going on. Besides, I'm not terribly fond of appearing on camera."

Jordan stopped at a yellow light, although he could have sped through. They were going to need to discuss his driving habits eventually. But for now his forehead was scrunched in thought. "Is it stage fright?" he asked. "You certainly seem comfortable with it, but I guess you could just be good at putting up a front."

"I don't have stage fright." He never had, not even as a boy, when he'd happily appeared in a series of school theater productions.

"Is it the makeup you hate? The hours? Or does the pay suck?"

It was a funny thing. People asked Landry questions all the time, mostly about what they should wear or what kind of crafts they could make out of dryer lint. Hardly anyone inquired about *him*—about what he felt and what he wanted. So Landry rewarded Jordan with the truth.

"I don't enjoy selling myself. I have good ideas to share, but I can do that in print. I don't like having to perform in order for people to listen to me."

Many people would have scoffed at this. In fact, Steve had urged Landry for years to get a show of his own, and when Landry dragged his feet, Steve had shaken his head. "You look fantastic on-screen, Lan, and it's the best way to promote your brand." He'd couldn't understand why Landry didn't want to leap more fully into showbiz.

Jordan, however, nodded thoughtfully. "I get it. You'd rather do stuff instead of acting like you're doing stuff."

And that was it, quite succinctly. "Yes," Landry said.

"You don't mind the guest bits with Suzee and the talk shows?"

"No, they're fine. Brief. They don't rule my life."

"Yeah, okay."

Traffic was grueling, and because Jordan followed Landry's instructions and avoided freeways, they crawled along surface streets. Jordan didn't seem to mind. His grip on the steering wheel didn't appear tense, and he didn't flip anyone off. In fact, sometimes when the car was immobile, he stroked the dashboard lovingly.

"This is the nicest set of wheels I've ever driven," he said. "Mostly I've had junkers when I owned a car at all. I had one piece of shit die on me while I was on the Alaskan Way Viaduct at rush hour. That was fun."

"What did you do?"

"Walked away. Which was stupid, because later I got a bigass towing bill for more than the car was worth." He sounded far more cheerful than the memory called for.

"Did you pay the towing bill?"

"Well, yeah, 'cause I didn't want the city or anyone coming after me. And it sucked because I lost my job since I couldn't get to work. That was one of the times I had to move back in with Mom and Dad."

Landry shuddered at the idea. He'd left home shortly after graduating high school and hadn't set foot in Nebraska since. But as soon as that thought crossed his mind, so did a flash of guilt over Missy's unread email, which remained in his inbox.

Thinking about Nebraska made him want to curl up in bed and binge-watch old sitcoms. And eat tacos. No—chimichangas. Stuffed with cheese and beef and smothered in sauce. With refried beans on the side and an oversize, salt-rimmed blended margarita.

"We haven't discussed meals," he said, probably more loudly than necessary.

"Want me to stop somewhere to pick up dinner?"

Yes, Landry wanted that very badly. But he shook his head. "I'll make something. What I meant is we haven't gone over the arrangements for when and where you'll take your meals."

"Oh. Well, I'm not picky. I can make myself sandwiches and soup and stuff in the pool house."

Jordan's apartment did have a kitchenette, but sandwiches and soup would be about the limit of what he could prepare. The refrigerator was tiny, as was the sink, and there was a two-burner stove and a microwave but no oven.

"Do you like to cook?" Landry asked.

"I've worked in enough restaurants that I can throw a few things together, but just basic stuff like burgers and spaghetti." He was stopped at a light and risked a quick glance Landry's way.

Landry thought carefully about how to word the next bit. It was a dangerous thing to offer, but his heart knew it was the right thing to do. "When I'm eating dinner at home, you're welcome to join me. If you like. It's not a job requirement unless we have urgent work to do."

Cue Jordan's familiar wide grin. "Really? Thanks! I'd like that. Eating alone sucks. Plus I've seen some of the recipes you come up with. Yum. Oh, unless you want me to cook."

Actually, that hadn't occurred to Landry. Elaine never prepared his meals. But then, she hadn't lived with him either. It would be convenient if someone else made dinner now and then. "Why don't you make something for tonight? Just make it quick since I have that reception at eight."

"Sure!"

When they arrived home, Jordan headed straight for the kitchen while Landry went to his study. After several minutes of dithering, and in an attempt to quell his curiosity over what Jordan was doing, Landry read and responded to a long list of messages. Then, finally, he reopened Missy's email.

> *Hi Wormy,*
> *The twins just got over a cold which means now it's my turn, and the house is practically knee-deep in used tissues. Gross. At least Rod hasn't caught it yet. He's a bigger baby than the twins when he gets sick. Tiny little cold and you'd think he's dying of the plague. I was pregnant with twelve pounds worth of babies and I didn't whine as much as he does over a sniffle.*
> *You know Wes Brunken who used to manage the Dairy Queen? Well, he*

*quit his job and ran off with Carlene
Hansen. Did you know her? She was
in my grade at school and she used
to work for the city doing billing and
stuff, but she quit a while back. I
forget why. Anyway, the two of them
were both married to other people,
but they ran off to Rapid City together.
Good thing neither of them had
kids, and from what I hear Carlene's
husband was kind of relieved, but
Wes's wife is real broken up over it.
Plus Wes is way too old for Carlene. I
think so, anyway.*

*Oh, and speaking of locals, did
you hear about Jaxon Powers? I know
he was a few years older than you but
you totally had a crush on him even
before he became a rock star, didn't
you? Anyway, there was some big spy
thing that happened with him in some
country in Eastern Europe. He got shot
and everything. But now he's giving a
huge pile of cash to Peril schools for
their arts programs. Who would've
thought someone from little old Peril
would be so famous and important? I
guess you have to step up your game
if you're going to be Peril's #1 most
famous person. Hahahaha. LOL.*

*Aunt Trudy's been working on
some kind of top secret project. She
won't say what. You know how she is.
But I'm giving you warning cause I*

*think the project's going to involve all
of us, and especially you, and if you
don't cooperate none of the rest of
us are ever going to hear the end of
it. I know Peril's not very interesting
compared to Hollywood, and I know
we're not exciting like your movie star
friends, but we're still family, Landry
Francis Bishop. So don't let us down.*
   XO,
   Missy

By the time Landry finished reading the email, his head hurt. It didn't help that he'd heard Missy's voice in his head, loud as ever, and he'd felt the ghost of a childhood bruise where she used to punch his arm when she didn't get her way. He'd tried telling on her, but since he was older by two years, their parents always took her side.

He didn't care about Wes Brunken and Carlene Hansen and didn't know why Missy thought he would. Yes, he'd harbored a slight crush on Jaxon Powers, who'd been an incredible musician even as a teenager. And he *had* heard about the "spy thing," although he'd paid it little attention since it happened shortly after Steve's death and had nothing to do with Landry. As for Aunt Trudy…. He sighed. Maybe she'd get distracted from her mysterious project. Right. And maybe the entire NFL would start playing in pink tutus.

Landry was still glaring at his laptop when Jordan rapped on the doorframe. "Um, dinner's ready."

"Okay." Landry stood.

"Should I not interrupt you when you're in your study?"

"Only if I say so explicitly."

"Cool."

The kitchen was a minor disaster area, with pots and bowls everywhere and an assortment of splatters on the counters and floor. Landry pretended not to see any of that as Jordan led him through to the dining room.

"I'll clean up later, don't worry," said Jordan.

Jordan had spread a pale green cloth over the table, and even though it was sized incorrectly—the dining room table could seat twelve, and this particular cloth was made for the much smaller kitchen table—it created an intimate eating area for two. He'd laid out matching green napkins and a pair of white place mats. He'd chosen the Waterford china—which Landry used only on holidays—and the best silverware.

"Is it okay?" Jordan was bouncing anxiously on the balls of his feet. "You have a lot of stuff and I wasn't sure what to use."

Landry gave a reassuring smile. "It's fine."

"Great! Uh, have a seat and I'll serve." Landry waited for Jordan to reappear with food, which didn't take long. He hurried back with a platter in one hand and a pair of bowls cradled in the other arm. He demonstrated his waiter's skills by getting everything to the table without spilling or dropping anything. Then he sat opposite Landry. "Dig in!"

With some trepidation, Landry did. The lettuce salad, torn into perfectly sized pieces, was heavily dressed with balsamic vinegar, sprigs of parsley, and whole sage leaves. A puzzling citrus-and-tomato-flavored red sauce with some lethal bits of chili pepper covered slightly soggy pasta. Landry choked and tried to counter the chilies with a glass of water, even though he knew that wasn't the best remedy. The beautifully tender chicken breast swam in a white sauce sporting little green flecks and pale lumps that proved to be chopped raw garlic.

Eventually Landry looked across the table to discover Jordan poking at his own still-full plate. "This is horrible," Jordan said. "I'm sorry."

"The salad is, um…."

"Barely edible. Yeah." A deep sigh.

Now was a time for gentle words. "What exactly were you aiming for here?"

"I was trying for fancy. I'm pretty good at cooking simple, easy-to-digest food for invalids, but I figured you didn't want boring, plain stuff."

"Well, it's not plain. Or boring."

Jordan snorted. "It's also not fit for human consumption. I'm sorry." His words seemed sincere, and a hint of amusement danced in his eyes, as if he was willing to joke about his culinary disaster.

"I appreciate the effort." That was honest.

"I tried some recipes I found on Zane Zafra's website. He's supposed to be a famous chef, right? I must have screwed up."

Landry snorted. "I wouldn't count on it. Zafra's nothing but a… a media monkey. He's good at playing up drama for the camera and he always looks pretty, but I doubt he could manage boxed macaroni and cheese. He probably makes up his recipes by randomly choosing food words, and then he acts like it's his followers' fault when the recipes fail."

"Yeah?" Jordan had broken out into a full-fledged grin. "I should have picked some of your recipes instead."

Landry ignored the tickly, warm feeling he got from Jordan's words. "Perhaps next time you should attempt something simpler. Or better yet, I'll do the cooking."

Tracing patterns in the pasta sauce with his spoon, Jordan nodded. "Maybe that's better. You're not pissed off at me?"

Oddly, Landry wasn't. Sure, the meal was appalling, but Jordan had *tried* to please him, and that counted for a great deal. "I've given advice several times about what to do when a project fails. You laugh about it, make do as best as you can, and learn from your mistakes. Nobody has ever died from a botched craft or a spoiled dinner."

Jordan's sunny smile reappeared. "Unless the craft involved explosives and the dinner had botulism."

"Fortunately, neither is the case here. I'll tell you what. You clean up and I'll make us sandwiches. I have to get ready for the reception soon."

"Deal."

As they worked together in the kitchen, Landry found himself smiling. Jordan was a cheerful presence, and Landry couldn't remember the last time anyone had shared kitchen duties with him. Although Elaine had sampled whatever Landry prepared, she didn't pitch in. It was nice to work alongside someone like this and have him grin at you as he mopped up a puddle of red sauce on the floor. And if that someone had merry blue eyes and soft-looking hair that Landry wanted to run his fingers through? Well, that shouldn't have been important, and yet it was.

They sat at the kitchen table to eat their sandwiches. No fine linens or china, just everyday ceramic plates, plain white cloth napkins, and a view of the lit-up pool.

"This is great," Jordan said after a few bites. "Really good bread. I like the spread too."

"There's more in a jar in the refrigerator if you want it later."

"Thanks. I should've just… I should've known better than to try to impress Landry Bishop in the kitchen."

"You did impress me. You made a sincere effort on my behalf."

"I'm just glad I didn't get myself fired."

"That will require more than a bad dinner. Not that it's something you should aspire to, of course." Landry took a sip of his iced tea and suddenly wished he could stay home tonight. He would put on a movie— something classic, like Hitchcock—and relax in the living room, and perhaps Jordan might want to watch with him. They could eat popcorn.

But that was a silly fantasy.

Jordan leaned forward and caught Landry's gaze. "I just wanted to impress you, I guess. To let you know I think you're… special. I don't have bad taste, you know. Like that sweater? I could tell that it matched your eyes. You must look amazing in it."

Under other circumstances, Landry would have assumed this was a flirtation. Or maybe he just wanted to believe it was, because Jordan was handsome and unexpectedly easy to spend time with.

More abruptly than he'd intended, Landry stood. "I need to change. We'll leave for the reception in thirty minutes."

Jordan, sitting with the remains of a sandwich, watched him go.

Chapter Six

A WEEK after Elaine left, Landry woke up early with plans to write all day. But since he needed some exercise first, he spent an hour in his home gym, riding his stationary bike while watching the morning talk shows. Sweaty and a little achy, he startled when Jordan appeared just as Landry was leaving the room.

"Here," Jordan said, holding out a frosted glass of clear liquid. "Hydrate."

Landry took the glass and had a careful sip. "Cucumber water?" he asked, surprised.

"Yeah. Is it okay? I used your recipe. Looked it up on your blog. Don't worry—I'm sticking to the easy stuff."

That was unexpected, but nice. Landry took a much longer swallow and then smiled at him. "It's perfect. Thank you."

"Would you rather have regular water after a workout? I noticed you don't usually use much ice, so I added only a couple of cubes, but I can change that too."

"This is fine." Landry was positive that nobody on the planet had ever paid attention to his ice preferences. He quelled the twinge of warm pleasure that Jordan *had* paid attention to such a small detail—and also the tingle that Jordan's close presence was causing on Landry's skin.

Neither of them moved. It should have been an awkward moment, the two of them silent in the hallway and only inches apart. But it wasn't. Jordan's Seattle-pale skin had already picked up some California tan, and his hair had new blond highlights from the sun. As far as Landry knew, Jordan never wore cosmetics, yet his lips were as plump and pink and tempting as a lipstick model's.

Belatedly, Landry realized he was licking his own lips. He took a hasty gulp of cucumber water, but it did nothing to cool him down. When he saw Jordan respond by—apparently unconsciously—licking his own lips, Landry nearly came undone.

"I need to shower," he said hoarsely.

"I, uh, okay. Sure. While you're doing that, how about if I make some eggs and a fruit salad, which I promise I can do without a disaster. You could maybe eat it poolside?"

"I have work to do." *Yes. Remember that. Much to accomplish today, and this tempting man is your employee.*

"But you have to eat. I bet if you have a decent breakfast you'll be a lot more productive."

He did have a point. "All right." And then, as if the words were desperate to escape: "Will you join me?"

Jordan's smile was stunning. "I'd love to."

Landry sped through his shower, and for once he skimped on his skin-care regime. He'd make sure to exfoliate tonight. He put a minimum of fuss into his hair as well, and then he dressed in salmon-colored linen trousers and a cream polo shirt with a bright snake embroidered along the collar. He couldn't explain why his chest felt fluttery as he made his way toward the patio. It was just breakfast with his PA, for God's sake.

Jordan, standing in front of the stove, shot him a grin. "Eggs are just about up. I'll meet you outside." The kitchen was in slight disorder, but Landry had confidence that Jordan would tidy it after they ate.

The sun seemed especially bright, but Jordan had set things up in the shade of a wide blue umbrella. The table held pastel madras place mats and napkins, simple everyday cutlery, and glasses of orange juice and cucumber water. A glass bowl sat heaped with cut fruit and covered by another napkin. Jordan had even grabbed a small potted orchid from the dining room and placed it on the table.

Smiling, Landry took his seat.

Only a minute or two later, Jordan hurried out with their plates. Simple scrambled eggs, done to perfection, and tiny piles of minced herbs from the pots on the kitchen windowsill. "Hope you don't mind mixing in your own," he said as he sat down. "I didn't want to create seasoning Armageddon."

"You got that idea from my blog too."

Jordan's teeth flashed white. "Yep."

They ate in silence, but there was an odd familiarity to it, as if it were something they'd been doing for years. A hummingbird buzzed past on its way to a bottlebrush plant, the pool sparkled, and a jet hummed overhead. A feeling of disconnect suddenly hit Landry, rocking him so hard that he had to put his fork down. How did weird Wormy Bishop from Peril, Nebraska, end up in an LA mansion with a beautiful man who seemed to want little more than to make him happy? What if it was all just a dream, and he'd wake up in his parents' old house and trudge his way to his salesclerk job at Svoboda Home and Ranch?

"Eggs okay?" Jordan asked softly, as if he didn't want to startle Landry. He looked concerned.

"Everything's fine. I'm glad you talked me into a poolside breakfast. Thank you."

Jordan leaned back in his seat, his expression satisfied. "I'm glad you took me up on the offer. You know, if you wanted to make a habit of this, we could multitask. While we eat, you could give me a rundown on what you need from me that day. Then we could both get to work as soon as we're well fed."

That was an excellent idea. Although Landry did wonder how many mornings he could endure sitting in the sweet sunshine with Jordan almost within reach. What if, one of these days, Landry couldn't stop himself? What if he ignored the cucumber water and grabbed Jordan instead?

Discipline, Landry Bishop. You can do this.

"I think we can try that," he said in what he hoped was an even tone. "It's a good suggestion."

Jordan smiled. And then something shifted in his expression. His mouth fell slightly open as his eyes widened, and a light flush colored his cheeks. "Click," he whispered. "Oh my God. Definitely a click."

"What?"

Still appearing a bit dazed, Jordan shook his head and stood. "Nothing. Do you want some coffee?" He started clearing the dishes.

Landry felt a bit shaken himself, although he couldn't say why. Maybe cucumber water had mild psychoactive effects. He stood as well. "No, thank you. But perhaps you could bring me some iced tea in an hour or so."

For once Jordan was unsmiling, his face almost deadly earnest. "I'll bring you whatever you need."

Landry, trying to ignore the hammering of his heart, gathered his remaining resolve and fled.

THAT afternoon Elaine called. Landry was in the middle of writing a guest blog on creative ways to make wrapping paper, but he didn't mind the interruption.

"You haven't panicked," said Elaine.

"How would you know? You're in Hawaii."

"I would have heard you from here."

He wished she could see his scowl. "I'm not hysterical."

"Not usually, no. But there was that time Todd spilled merlot on you."

"He spilled it on my cream-colored cashmere blazer three minutes before the *Suzee Show* went on-air. I looked like a murder victim." In retrospect, Landry shouldn't have trusted Todd with the wine to begin with. The stagehand was pretty, but he had all the grace of a drunken giraffe, plus a tendency to wave his hands when excited. Apparently he'd been very excited over Landry's upcoming segment on things to make out of wine bottle corks. Landry had nearly burst into tears over the spill, but Elaine had been standing nearby and fortunately suggested an impromptu bit on stain removal.

Now, Landry kept his voice regal. "I'm perfectly calm."

"Good. Does that mean Jordan's working out?"

"Yes, I've been letting him use my home gym."

"Oh my God. Was that a joke? Did Landry Bishop attempt a pun?"

He glared at the phone again. "I'm often witty."

"Uh-huh. So, Jordan. He's a keeper?"

Landry knew Jordan wasn't eavesdropping. He was, in fact, using Landry's writing time as an opportunity to take a break from his own tasks, which probably meant he was in the pool. He swam often, and if Landry snuck a few peeks at the beautiful, skimpily clad man doing laps, well, he was only human. Besides, Jordan had had a full week to purchase bathing attire, if he so desired. He didn't seem inclined.

"Landry?"

He reeled his thoughts back to the conversation. "We've had some rough spots, but he's learning quickly. He'll do, I guess."

"So I was right and you were wrong." Her smugness traveled thousands of miles, undiminished.

A redirection was in order. "Have you settled in all right?"

"More or less. I forgot how much my parents drive me insane. I love them. They're great. But they make me crazy. Sometimes they act like I'm still thirteen. The other day I said *fuck* in front of Mom and she told me to watch my language. I was like, 'What're you gonna do, ground me?'" Elaine huffed. "It's okay, though. Our place has a nice lanai, so when I can't stand it one second longer I can sit out there with a mai tai and remember I'm living in paradise. But really, Landry. How are you doing?"

"No mai tais. No lanais. It's not paradise. But it is the city of angels, and that's close enough."

They chatted a few minutes longer about nothing consequential. For some time after the call ended,

Landry remained in his chair, thinking about what Elaine had said about her parents. His own were long gone—his father died of a heart attack when Landry was in high school, and cancer took his mother soon after. Neither of them had lived long enough to see him become successful. He wasn't sure what they would have made of him. Maybe in their eyes he'd always have remained weird little Wormy, the bookworm who cared more about fashion magazines than football.

He still had Missy, though. And her husband and kids, along with a slew of aunts and uncles and cousins, all of whom were apparently content to live out their lives in the middle of nowhere. His relatives weren't horrible people, but when Landry was a kid, they'd driven him nuts—and there'd been no lanai to retire to with a tropical drink.

Landry had never bothered to come out since he'd never been in. By the time he'd hit his teens, it was already crystal clear to everyone that he was gay. Not a single relative had hassled him over it, and his cousins threatened anyone at school who dared to bully him. But Landry had always felt like an alien among them, a changeling child who never quite fit in.

"Which is why I am here in Los Angeles," he reminded himself aloud. Where he *did* fit in—even if it took some effort—and where he was supposed to be working on the blog post and not angsting over his childhood.

But although he rested his fingers on the keyboard, not a single word came. He couldn't think of anything clever to say about wrapping paper. Or anything else. Maybe he needed a change of scenery. He hadn't taken a vacation in forever. Hawaii. Landry could go to Hawaii. He would *not* stalk Elaine. Instead he'd rent a nice little place on a sugar-sand beach, watch surfers flex their muscles as they rode the waves, and eat fresh pineapple and papaya for breakfast. Then he'd come up with a series of blog posts on how to inject tropical touches into everyday life even if you lived in Duluth, and that meant he'd be able to write off the entire trip. An excellent plan all around.

Landry would have started clicking immediately, buying plane tickets and booking a rental house, but he decided to wait until Jordan got out of the pool. It would be a good chance to teach him how to make travel arrangements. Besides, Landry needed to discuss Jordan's preferences. When Elaine had accompanied Landry on trips, she'd arranged for them to have separate rooms on the same hotel floor. But if Landry was going to rent a house in Hawaii, would Jordan feel comfortable staying there? Or would be prefer his own place? What if Jordan wanted to hook up with someone while they were there? Landry wasn't sure how he felt about that, but it didn't seem fair to lug his PA to Hawaii and demand he remain celibate.

Come to think of it, they hadn't yet discussed whether Jordan could have dates over at the pool house, had they?

Landry laid his head in his arms and whimpered.

He was still in that position—and contemplating taking a nap for the first time in years—when his phone announced a new text message. Bleary-eyed, he read the message from the *Suzee Show*'s producer, which was really long. Suzee's mother needed surgery the following week, meaning Suzee would be unable to tape her show. Generally that wouldn't be a problem, but with the holiday season nearly upon them and guests already booked, delays would make a mess. Could Landry guest host for a few days?

It wasn't his favorite gig, but he'd done it before, and he owed Suzee a solid. She'd been one of the first people to give him an audience back when all he had was a blog, and she'd championed him from the start.

Sure, I can do that, he texted back.

Well, there went those Hawaii plans. It didn't seem worthwhile to fly all the way to the islands when he'd have to turn around and come home before his jet lag had even resolved. Instead of mourning his loss of paradise, he decided to plan a more manageable trip. Something in the Pacific time zone but outside of LA, where the weather wouldn't be too awful. Palm Desert? No.

Vegas! Just a few hours away by car, so no need to hassle with airports, and the entire place was ridiculous enough that he'd forget to take himself too seriously, at least for a few days. He could research some hot new restaurants. And he wouldn't have to face the question of where to put Jordan, because in Vegas they'd be staying at a hotel instead of in a house.

By the time Jordan appeared in Landry's doorway, fully dressed but with wet hair, Landry had made up his mind. "Vegas," Landry said.

Jordan blinked. "Um… what?"

"We're going to Las Vegas. Tomorrow."

"Really?" Jordan's face lit up like a boy who'd been told he was going to Disneyland. "With shows and slot machines and neon lights?"

"Las Vegas has those things."

"Cool! What's the occasion?"

"Escaping LA." Landry shrugged. "Temporarily, at any rate. Investigating eating establishments. And it'll give you practice making travel arrangements."

"Great!"

Landry carried his laptop to the kitchen table, where Jordan sat beside him—close enough that Landry felt the warmth of his body—notepad and pencil in hand, the world's most enthusiastic student.

"The first step," Landry intoned, "is transportation. Elaine sent you the file with my airline and flight preferences, right?"

"She did. Hey, is first class really worth all the extra bucks?"

"Yes. Especially on longer flights. It gives me room to work." Landry made a mental note to ensure Jordan got to experience first class himself, sometime soon. His delight would more than offset the cost. "But this time we'll be driving."

Jordan literally bounced in his seat. "I get to take the Benz on open highway? Um, unless you want to drive."

"The pleasure can be all yours." Landry would be prepping for the *Suzee Show* along the way.

That settled, they discussed lodging. Landry's initial idea had been adjoining suites, but as he scrolled down the hotel's website, Jordan pointed at a photo of a two-bedroom suite. "Why can't we do that instead? It's cheaper and has more space."

"Wouldn't you prefer more privacy?"

"The only other times I was in Vegas, me and, like, six other guys shared one room. Everyone was drunk all the time and a couple of the guys ended up bringing girls back to the room, and... let's just say it was educational." He grinned merrily. "Anyway, I'd have my own room in this suite, plus my own bathroom that looks bigger than my first apartment. That's plenty of privacy for me. Is it enough for you?"

Actually, Landry had been thinking it would be nice to share a space with Jordan—not that two thousand square feet was exactly intimate. "It will be convenient to have you close," he said, hating the stiffness of his own voice.

Jordan dropped his voice and leaned nearer, making sure to catch Landry's gaze. "Close is good."

Ignoring that enigmatic comment, Landry booked the suite for three nights. Then, with Jordan watching closely, he emailed the concierge with a list of dinner reservation requests.

"What about show tickets?" asked Jordan.

Landry waved a hand dismissively. "I've seen all the ones that interest me. The Cirques, Absinthe, Elton John…. If you want to see something, just contact the concierge and have the ticket charged to my account."

Looking disappointed, Jordan shook his head. "No fun alone." Then he tipped his head to the side and gazed appraisingly at Landry. "What if I arrange one entertainment thing for us both? Something maybe you haven't already seen?"

"No Chippendales. Or strippers of any gender."

"Fair enough."

They covered other details, such as when they'd leave and when they'd return and what items they'd need to pack. Jordan took a lot of notes and asked good questions, which Landry found promising. He hated all the details of making travel arrangements and really hoped Jordan would be up to the task in the future.

When everything was settled to Landry's satisfaction, he stood. Before returning to his office with the laptop, though, he paused. "This is meant to be a vacation, and while I'll expect your assistance part of the time, you shouldn't feel as if you're tethered to me permanently. Feel free to go out and have some fun."

Jordan looked up at him, his expression uncharacteristically serious. "I'd rather stick close and make sure you're happy. *That*'s what I want to do."

Unsure how to respond to that, Landry nodded stiffly and walked away.

TRAFFIC was light once they hit the 15, but despite Jordan's delight about driving, he kept within a few miles of the speed limit. Landry let him choose what to listen to along the way, which meant a steady stream of P!nk, Britney, and Lady Gaga. None of which was especially to Landry's taste, but the music so clearly made Jordan happy that Landry didn't complain. Sometimes Jordan sang along, while other times he seemed content to smile at the road in front of them, commenting occasionally on things he saw.

"Those are Joshua trees, right? I've seen pictures but never met one in person. The other times I went to Vegas we flew in, so I didn't get to see the desert for real. Wow, they totally look like something out of a Dr. Seuss book."

Landry glanced up from his laptop, where he'd been sketching out a *Suzee Show* segment on decorating jack-o'-lanterns with glitter. Halloween would arrive soon, and he'd had to set aside the Thanksgiving, Christmas, and New Year's projects he'd been working on.

"Joshua trees," he confirmed. He'd forgotten how strange they'd looked to him the first time he spied one.

"Yeah. Cool. You know, I used to think deserts were all either the kind with camels and sand dunes or the kind with sagebrush and cowboys. But there's a lot of stuff out here, isn't there? Lots of different plants and rocks and things. Plus all these weird little towns. What

do you suppose leads people to live way out here?"
They had just passed an Air Force base and the borax
mine. "Jobs, I assume. And some people prefer to live
more isolated." He thought of the Nebraska Sandhills
near Peril, where a person could easily go days without
seeing another human, if he so desired. Where traffic
jams and strip malls and blaring sirens were hundreds
of miles away, and where the land and sky stretched to
infinity. Where you could sit for hours hearing nothing
but the wind and a few birds, and where you didn't
have an image to maintain.

Jordan sounded thoughtful when he spoke next.
"I'm not sure I could hack it. Not unless I had someone
to share the solitude with. Then maybe I'd be okay. I'd
still miss rain, though."

They lapsed back into silence, and Landry returned
his attention to pumpkins. Or tried to, anyway. He was
suddenly much too aware that Jordan was right there,
only inches away, and that he smelled of chlorine
and sugar—from his morning swim and breakfast,
respectively. It was a pleasant scent, like the ghost of
those long-ago summers when Landry and Missy and
an assortment of cousins sat near the Peril community
pool with Popsicles dripping onto their skin.

Popsicles. In late spring, he'd do a blog post on
frozen fruit treats for grown-ups. He made a note on his
phone so he wouldn't forget.

Traffic grew increasingly heavy as soon as they
crossed the Nevada border, but Jordan remained
cheerful. He exclaimed over the solar farm and casino
roller coaster in Primm and laughed at the string of
Vegas-related billboards.

When they reached their hotel—a newer property
on the Strip—Jordan insisted on carrying all the luggage,

even though Landry was perfectly capable of wheeling his own bag. "I'm your PA. I think part of my job entails making sure you arrive like a proper celebrity."

Although Landry snorted, he was secretly charmed by Jordan's enthusiasm.

Landry steered them into the exclusive lounge reserved for the hotel's highest-paying guests, where an employee offered them wine as she checked them in. They both declined, although Landry had a mineral water with lime instead.

A private elevator served only the floors containing the upscale suites. "Wow, swanky," Jordan commented as they rose.

When they reached the suite itself, he just stood and gaped. "Holy crap!"

"What?"

"It's… like something out of a movie." Jordan swept his arm toward the wall of windows. "I mean, that view! Wow! And the rest." He did a slow spin, no doubt taking in the expansive living and dining areas, the wet bar, the television screens big enough to be seen from Mars.

"It's a nice property," Landry agreed. He waited near the entryway, smiling, while Jordan explored. Predictably, Jordan exclaimed over the enormous bathrooms—the suite had two, plus a powder room—with high-end toiletries and bouquets of fresh flowers. But what truly sent him over the edge was the discovery that the lights, drapes, thermostats, and televisions were all controlled from tablets strategically placed throughout. He spent a good five minutes opening and closing things and turning things on and off.

Finally Jordan set down the tablet and gave Landry a sheepish smile. "Sorry."

"It's fine."

"It's dorky. Suffice it to say, the rooms my buddies and I shared at Casa de Jackpot weren't anything like this."

"I didn't always stay in luxury hotels either." His family had gone on road trips each summer, sometimes to the nearby Black Hills and sometimes farther. His parents liked visiting national parks, which was fine, but they'd cram everyone into the cheapest motel rooms they could find and insist it was all part of the adventure. Landry had grown jaded since then, taking all the amenities for granted. He was glad that Jordan reminded him how fortunate he was.

Landry cleared his throat. "I'm going to do some work. You can—"

"I thought you were on vacation."

"We'll have a nice dinner out tonight."

"Yeah, okay, but what about until then?" Jordan hovered close, his expression hopeful.

"Go out and enjoy yourself. I'll text if I need anything." Ignoring Jordan's disapproving look, Landry set up his laptop on a desk facing the windows. He'd have nice scenery while he typed.

Jordan didn't go anywhere, at least not right away. He took the suitcases to their respective bedrooms and, judging from the sounds, tucked the clothing away in drawers and closets. After he emerged into the living room, he collapsed onto a couch, where he spent some time perusing tourism magazines.

Landry continued to type. Having finalized his jack-o'-lantern plans, he brainstormed questions for some of the guests he'd have to interview on the *Suzee Show*. Suzee's producer would help him with this task, but Landry wanted to contribute. He had no trouble finding things to ask an assortment of musicians and actors but came up short when he realized one guest was an Olympic skier.

"Do you know anything about skiing?"

Jordan looked up from his magazine. "I didn't know that was an option in Vegas."

"It isn't. It's for the *Suzee Show*."

"Oh. Well, sorry. I was never into paying money to freeze my ass off while hurtling down a mountain. But if you want safer sports, there's a place here where you can pay to drive sports cars around a race track. Or we could do a little hike at Red Rock Canyon. That's only a half hour from here." He held up the magazine as if providing proof.

"Go ahead if you want."

Jordan huffed before tossing the magazine aside and standing. "I think I'm gonna just go watch the dancing fountains and stuff." He walked slowly to the door, paused, and looked back at Landry. "Want anything while I'm out?"

"No thanks. Be back by six."

"Sure."

It should have been easier to work after Jordan left, but without him, the suite felt huge and empty, which was foolish. Landry wandered to the bank of windows and stared out at the flashing lights and crowded sidewalks. A Vegas-themed New Year's party. That could be a fun thing to blog about. But he was supposed to be working on questions for the *Suzee Show*.

Landry's stomach grumbled, reminding him he hadn't eaten all day. Dinner was still a long way off. He reached for one of the tablets, intending to order something from room service, but he stopped his hand in midair. He wasn't in the mood for overpriced gourmet fare. He wanted… something else. Something *real*.

It was always disorienting to traverse the casino floor in search of a way outdoors. Even though Landry had stayed here before, he took a few wrong turns before finally discovering a mall, which led to a skybridge, which led to one of those packed sidewalks he'd been watching from on high. He joined the throng—opting at random to go north—and for several long blocks he simply strolled along, ignoring the people who wanted to give him flyers advertising prostitutes.

When he saw a McDonald's, he skulked inside and stood in line behind a couple and their three young children. Two of the kids were whining, while the third napped in a stroller. The parents ignored their offspring, peering at their cell phones instead.

Landry bought a large order of fries and, clutching the fragrant bag, hurried outside and started his return route. He popped the treat into his mouth one at a time, savoring the heat and salt and grease. God, the fries tasted good!

Sometimes, back in high school, he used to join a group of cousins and friends at the Dairy Queen, Peril's only fast-food outlet. Everyone was supposed to be studying, but mostly they'd gossiped and teased and thrown straw wrappers at one another. Those were surprisingly good memories. Even though people considered Landry odd, he wasn't excluded from the group. In fact, some of the girls would show him their latest issues of *Seventeen* and seek his input on clothing or makeup.

His childhood hadn't been a fairy tale—but it hadn't been a horror story either.

He finished his snack shortly before arriving back at the hotel and furtively stuffed the empty bag into a trash can, like a man destroying evidence of a crime.

He strolled into the casino with a casual air, although his hands were messy. Had he been alone at home, he might have licked them clean, even if he'd have felt guilty about it. Here, he ducked into the nearest bathroom to wash up.

Back out on the casino floor, he briefly considered playing a few rounds of video poker or maybe dropping twenty bucks in a slot machine—perhaps the Ellen-themed one. But no, he had those shows to prep for, not to mention the book deadlines and blog entries and a day's backlog of emails. He headed up to his suite.

He'd just settled in front of the laptop when the door clicked open and Jordan entered, carrying a plastic bag.

"Bought swimming trunks," he said, striding toward his room. "I figured the resort isn't as forgiving as you about guys who take a dip in their Andrew Christians."

A series of dazzling images appeared instantly in Landry's head: Jordan doing laps, his strong legs and lovely ass breaching the surface of the water, thin bright fabric clinging to those tempting curves. Jordan floating on his back with eyes closed against the sun, only a scrap of material on that glistening skin. Jordan padding along the pool deck, droplets making him sparkle, then diving into the deep end.

Realizing that Jordan was staring at him from the bedroom doorway, Landry cleared his throat. "I thought you might have forgotten your promise to acquire proper bathing attire." He raised his eyebrows playfully.

"Nope. Been too busy before now. My boss is relentless—never gives me a moment's peace." He winked.

"Well, he's giving you time off now. Are you heading off to swim?"

"Sure. Join me?"

"I can't." Landry pointed to the laptop.

"Right. Work to do." Jordan's eyes sparkled as if he were in on a hilarious joke. "Did you interrupt your drudgery to have lunch, by the way? If not, I can bring you something. The Thai place downstairs does takeout."

"I, um, ate something."

"You sure?" Still amused, although Landry had no idea why.

"I'm fine. Go swim."

Once Jordan left, Landry was able to make some true progress on his to-do list. Even though he kept imagining Jordan moving through the hotel pool, body sleek and strong. He even read a new message from his sister.

> *Hey Wormy,*
>
> *We're having absolutely perfect weather right now with the temps turning just a little crisp, but you still only need a light jacket at night. The leaves on that big old oak tree in the backyard are starting to change color. Do you remember that time we climbed it even though we weren't supposed to, and you fell and hurt your ankle? You didn't want to tell Mom and Dad so you ended up trying to hide your limp for days.*
>
> *I ran into Ashley Neth at Barn Owl Market yesterday. You remember her—she used to be Ashley Myers until she got married. She was your year in school and always really full of herself. She wore her stupid*

*cheerleader outfit all over town when
she totally didn't have to, just showing
off, you know? She and her husband,
they have a little money because he's
a dentist, but his name is Seth Neth,
and that just goes to show none of
them have any sense at all.*

*Anyway, yesterday Ashley was
cooing at me because she saw you in
some magazine. Like, everybody already
knew you're famous, so I don't know
why she was acting like this was a
sudden revelation. I was mature, though.
I just smiled and didn't remind her what
a bitch she was to you in high school.*

*If snooty old Ashley Meyer Neth
thinks you're a big f'ing deal, can
you imagine what the rest of town
thinks? You really ought to make an
appearance here one of these days,
Wormy. Give us yokels a thrill.*

*Actually, you might have to show
up sooner than you think. I told you,
Aunt Trudy's got something up her
sleeve, and it involves you. Because
everyone thinks you're a pretty big
deal. Be warned.*

*You know, I'd kinda like to see
you too.*
XO,
Missy

He didn't know what to write back to her. He used
to tell her some of the funny things Steve had said,

because he could be really funny at the most unexpected times. That was a major reason Landry had fallen for him. But now? Missy had as much interest in industry gossip as Landry did in Ashley Neth, and Missy didn't want any of his décor or entertainment advice. He couldn't even justify talking about the weather, because the LA climate was boring. And he was tired of coming up with excuses to avoid Peril.

Landry ended up sending a bland little message about hiring a new PA and taking on some unexpected TV shows. He didn't mention how handsome Jordan was or how his presence made Landry's house feel more interesting, more alive. Then Landry simply asked her for photos of the twins. That would occupy her for a while.

Jordan bounded into the suite a few minutes after six. "Sorry I'm late!" he said, breathing hard. "Got to talking with some people poolside and lost track of time."

People? What people? God, that was absolutely none of Landry's business. "It's fine. We still have time. But we should get dressed now."

"Will you tell me if what I brought is okay?"

Landry agreed, which turned out to be a good thing. Jordan had packed his college-intern suit. It wouldn't have gotten him kicked out of the restaurant, but he could do much better. Landry shook his head. "Did you bring those skinny black jeans you wore the other day?"

Jordan grinned. "Yeah."

"Forget about the khakis and wear the jeans instead. The shirt will do"—a plain white button-down—"but I'm going to lend you a tie. And a jacket. It won't be a perfect fit, but it'll do for tonight. As for your shoes… well, I suppose they'll be hidden under the table."

If Jordan was offended, he certainly didn't show it. In fact, he smiled widely as he skinned off his now-dry swimming trunks. Landry tried not to stare as Jordan, gloriously naked, took his time apparently searching for the perfect pair of underwear.

But it was impossible to look away. Jordan's body was nicely toned but not over-muscled, with a sprinkling of pale hairs on his chest and lower belly—all of which Landry knew already, thanks to Jordan's swimming sessions at home. But now Jordan had revealed the portions previously covered by fabric, and, well…. Wow. Smooth, rounded buttocks that Landry yearned to caress, a barely trimmed bush, and a plump, soft cock a few shades pinker than the rest of him.

Jordan took his time putting underwear on, too, performing a de-stripping show that Landry found sexier than anything Vegas could offer.

"I'll be changing," said Landry, realizing he should have left the room already. "I'll be back shortly with a jacket and tie."

"Sure thing." Jordan was now searching for socks, it seemed.

Landry had to glare down an incipient hard-on before getting into his own black trousers. He went with a white shirt too—albeit better tailored than Jordan's—and a plain black tie. His blazer was also black, but the heavy black embroidery on the lapels and down the sleeves saved him from looking like an FBI agent. Well, that and the way he carefully sculpted his hair with product. G-men, he suspected, didn't bother with that.

He gave Jordan a gray tie and a more subdued black jacket, and although Jordan had done nothing to his hair but comb it into place, he looked gorgeous. Delicious, even.

"Passable?" Jordan asked.

Landry spared him a smile. "You'll do."

They took one of the hotel's chauffeured town cars, another perk of their high-class suite. Jordan seemed amused to sit in the back seat and let someone else drive.

Le Renard Violet was located in one of the city's newest properties, but not on the casino floor. To get to the restaurant, Landry and Jordan had to locate a special elevator tucked into a discreet corner, where an officious man checked Landry's name on his tablet before allowing them past.

"Fancy place, huh?" asked Jordan as the elevator rose.

"It's new and exclusive. I had to pull some strings to get reservations on such short notice."

"Is that the kind of thing you'll want me to do in the future?"

"Yes. When we return home, we can go over it."

The smiling hostess, clad in an evening gown, met them as soon as they disembarked. She led them through the dark, quiet dining room to a table beside a window, at which point she was seamlessly replaced by a young man who filled their water glasses.

Jordan leaned toward Landry and spoke in a stage whisper. "What's the decorating theme here? Alice in Wonderland shouts tallyho?"

Landry almost choked on his water, because Jordan had a point. Framed paintings featured fox hunters chasing oversize technicolor prey. "Lord Thistlebottom drops acid, I think."

"Lord who?"

"It's... sort of an inside joke with Elaine. That's what she calls me when she thinks I'm being pompous."

"Ah. I like it." Jordan lifted his water glass. "To Lord Thistlebottom!"

Smiling, Landry joined the toast.

But when they lowered their glasses, Jordan fixed him with a steady gaze. "You're not pompous, you know."

"I am."

"No. You're smart and you have a huge vocabulary. And you're *careful*. Um, mindful, maybe? Controlled. You're kind of remarkable, actually." And then Jordan bit his lip and looked away, as if he were stopping himself from saying more.

The menu was a five-course prix fixe with no choices. Diners were supposed to be grateful for whatever the chef's daily whim might be. Which was fine in principle, except today the chef seemed to have taken a random culinary lurch across continents.

"What's this?" Jordan asked when their first course arrived. Each plate sported a patty about the size of a silver dollar, with a sprinkling of microgreens and a tiny dollop of red sauce on the side.

"A curried crab and scallop cake." Landry had peeked at the menu after they sat down.

"Okay."

The cake wasn't bad, although the curry contained an overabundance of cinnamon and cardamom. The red sauce had something to do with pomegranates. Even attempting delicate nibbles, Landry finished off the entire thing in three bites.

The waiter had a heavy New Jersey accent. He tried to hide it, but not very successfully. Still, he was efficient about clearing away the plates and refilling their glasses.

"No wine." Jordan pointed at a few of the neighboring tables. "They all have wine, but we don't."

"I specified just water when I made the reservation."

"But you like wine, right?"

"I do, but I am quite satisfied without it." Absolutely true, and drinking in front of Jordan would have been somewhat rude.

"But I'm *your* PA. Shouldn't I be catering to your needs instead of the other way round?"

"I don't need wine."

For some reason that triggered Jordan's wide smile. He dropped the topic, gazing out the window at the spectacle below. "Have you been to the Neon Museum?" he asked after a moment.

"The what?"

"I read about it in that magazine in the room. They have a bunch of old signs from casinos and stuff, and you can go on tours. It sounds kind of cool."

"Do you want to go?"

Jordan shook his head. "The magazine said night tours sell out weeks in advance."

"I could try pulling some of those strings I was talking about."

"Being famous is kind of handy, isn't it?"

Landry was about to protest that he wasn't truly *famous*—he simply had good connections. But then the waiter brought the second course. Landry had to explain that one too. It was a miniature barigoule: a few tablespoons of artichoke bits braised with chopped garlic and bok choy, all in a creamy sauce spiked with chilies. It was more interesting than tasty. And gone in only four bites. God, he was hungry.

After the waiter whisked their plates away, Jordan looked wistfully at the table. "I guess this place is too fancy to give you bread, huh?"

"Much." A month after Steve had died, Landry had put on an old pair of jeans, a T-shirt he'd owned since college, and his most comfortable running shoes. Then he hopped into the Jag and drove to an Olive Garden in Bakersfield, where he hoped nobody would recognize him. He'd stuffed his face with breadsticks and felt emotionally stronger when he was done.

"Can I ask you something, Landry?"

"Of course."

"How did you end up being so successful? Not that you don't deserve it! You totally do. But how does a guy go from Peril, Nebraska, to nighttime talk shows?"

Oddly pleased that Jordan remembered the name of his hometown, Landry twisted the glass between his palms. "It was mostly good luck, actually."

"Yeah?"

"I'd known since I was young that I wanted a career in fashion or home design. Nebraska was clearly not the best place for that, so I went to college in Southern California."

"How did your family feel about that?"

Landry winced. "My father had passed away by then, and—"

"I'm so sorry!" Jordan looked pained, as if the loss were recent.

"Thank you. My mother knew Peril was no place for me. She insisted on using part of Dad's life insurance to help pay my tuition."

"Hooray for supportive parents!" Jordan raised his water glass in a salute.

Landry nodded. Even though she hadn't understood him at all, she had been supportive, and that had been a wonderful gift. "How about your family? Are they supportive too?"

Jordan chuckled. "Maybe too much. I think they kinda spoiled me. We weren't rich or anything—just solid middle class—but Mom and Dad have always made it clear that I can rely on them if I need to. Even when I'm way past old enough to be responsible for myself. They're part of the reason I needed to leave Seattle—it was time for this bird to finally leave the nest. But we were talking about *you*. About your mom."

"She died too," he said quietly. "Not long before I finished my degree. And she'd wanted so badly to see me graduate."

"You were left alone really young."

"Not alone; I have a sister. Plus, a good portion of Peril is related to me by blood or marriage."

The shadows fled Jordan's expression. "Hooray also for extended family. Like the ones who get you a fantastic job with an amazing boss." He winked.

"I'm not amazing."

For once Jordan appeared completely serious. "You totally are, Landry."

Landry pretended to be fascinated by the view.

The waiter saved him by bringing the third course, which consisted of two tablespoons of couscous arranged into a tiny mountain, topped by a flag made of chive and red pepper. A thin line of brown sauce formed a crooked path up the side of the mountain, while a tiny puddle of blue corn gruel constituted a pond at the mountain's base.

Jordan bent to peer closely at his plate. "Wow. Geography for dinner."

"The chef's famous for his edible landscapes."

"Well, of course he is!"

Unfortunately this landscape was bland, and the pathway—which tasted of fish sauce—clashed with the spices in the pond. Plus the whole thing was only a few spoonsful. Now Landry understood the Wonderlandesque aspect of the restaurant décor: the longer the meal went on here, the hungrier he became. It was a fate that seemed fitting for the Red Queen, perhaps.

At least the water wasn't served in thimbles.

The waiter took away their empty plates with a flourish, as if he were performing a magic trick.

"This would be a good place for people whose eyes really are bigger than their stomach," Jordan said. "But okay. At the end of the last episode, you'd just graduated from college. How did you get from there to here?"

Landry admired Jordan's tenacity, but he reminded himself that the trait could prove dangerous. If Jordan pushed for a closer relationship, Landry doubted his own ability to resist.

"I got jobs. Low-level management in retail and hospitality at first. But it was LA, and our customers tended toward rich and famous. It was a good way to learn a lot and get noticed. Soon I had the chance to do some merchandising, designing window displays and that sort of thing."

"I bet you nailed that job."

"I suppose so. Then I started some things on the side. This was a decade ago, so social media wasn't the same as today, but I had a blog. I collected some influential followers." He shrugged to downplay the facts, but in truth, he'd been wild with excitement at the time. "Some of them began to hire me as, well, an event planner of sorts. Not for huge occasions such as weddings, but for smaller affairs. A dinner party hosted by a director, a pool party hosted by an up-and-coming actress. That sort of thing."

"Wow. That must have been thrilling."

"For this kid from Nebraska? You bet."

"And it all snowballed from there?"

Landry could have nodded and left it that, and he wouldn't exactly be lying. But it wouldn't be honest either. And thus far his relationship with his new PA had been honest—about almost everything.

"I had help," Landry said softly.

Jordan waited, not saying anything, but with his attention focused so sharply on Landry that the rest of Vegas might as well have not existed. He seemed to truly *care*. His hand rested on the tabletop only a few inches from Landry's.

"I met Steve," Landry continued. "His law firm hired me to plan an event for some of their clients. Cocktails, finger foods, semiformal attire. Most of their clients are in the industry, so it was a glittery crowd."

"And you fell for Steve instead of an actor?"

Landry couldn't help but smile at the memory. "The actors hadn't shown up yet; the party wouldn't start for an hour. I was running around, trying to make sure everything was going according to plan. It was an important gig for me. Then this attorney pulls me aside and demands a cost comparison of the crab puffs I'd ordered with the shrimp puffs he thought would be cheaper. He wasn't thrilled with the wine price points either."

At the table nearest them, a man and woman burst into raucous laughter. But Jordan didn't spare them a glance, keeping his gaze on Landry's face. "That was sexy? Arguing with you?"

"Actually, I suppose it was. Well, Steve was sexy, period. And he was good at arguing. As passionate about making a point as I was about dressing well. I liked that, even if we disagreed over the menu. We took our discussion to his office for privacy's sake and... things escalated fast." His face heated, and he wasn't sure if it was embarrassment or recalled desire. He'd barely been one to kiss on the first date, let alone strip naked in an office on Wilshire Boulevard. But Steve had pushed all the right buttons from the very beginning, in a way nobody else ever had.

Until Jordan.

Shit.

Apparently oblivious to Landry's sudden inner turmoil, Jordan leaned forward. "So that was it, huh? Love at first sight?"

"Lust, anyway," Landry said. "Steve was twenty years older than me, and we got censure from both sides. Everyone assumed I was a gold digger and that he was a cradle robber. But it wasn't his money I cared about. I fell for *him*."

"I've seen his picture in your study. He was really handsome."

"He was. He was also brilliant and focused, and when I went on about Eero Saarinen's designs or the advantages of Meyer lemons over Eureka, Steve listened. He wanted to hear what I had to say. He didn't always agree with me, but that was good too." He took a deep breath and let it out slowly. "We planned our life together. Steve introduced me to Suzee's producer, which was my big break, and to a couple of literary agents. He was convinced I could be a star."

"And now you are."

"In a small way, I suppose."

The fourth course arrived just then, and it was beautiful. Each plate contained a slice of extremely rare beef approximately the same dimensions as a playing card—thickness and all—along with three little dots of sauce, each a different color. A single teeny-tiny carrot and a marble-size potato completed the presentation.

"Somewhere in Vegas," Jordan said, contemplating his dish, "a pair of elves is enjoying our rightful meal. Or fairies."

"Tinker Bell?"

"Yes. Tinker Bell has a hot date, and right this moment they're eating *our* delicious, juicy cheeseburgers with curly fries and cookies 'n cream shakes. Then they're going to head over to New York-New York and see *Zumanity*, after which they'll get blitzed on comped Jack Daniels at the five-dollar blackjack table."

Landry covered his mouth to hold in his laughter. A snort escaped anyway, which was a little mortifying, except then Jordan guffawed in response. The couple at the next table—the same ones who'd been cackling like hyenas a few minutes ago—stared.

"I bet old Tink is skilled at cards," Landry said between chortles.

"Old Tink *counts* cards, in fact. But she's really good at it. Casino security's had their eye on her for years but haven't managed to catch her at it. She spends her winnings on convertibles and beachside condos. But she also has a little problem—fairy dust, you know—and she's been in and out of rehab several times."

"Poor thing."

"Yeah," Jordan said solemnly. "But now she's finally gotten over the whole Peter thing, so that's good. Her future is bright."

"I hope she's enjoying our dinner."

The beef was actually delicious, but so ephemeral it nearly melted on the tongue.

When the table was cleared once again, Landry realized they'd been sitting there for a long time and he hadn't once had the urge to check his texts or emails. Not only that. He hadn't once given a thought to future

TV show segments or blog entries or to his pending book deadlines. And he hadn't been overcome with grief when discussing Steve. Instead, he felt more relaxed than he had in ages.

He leaned back in his chair. "Thank you."

"For what?"

"Humoring me."

"I didn't know I was."

Landry waved a hand vaguely. "We both know this isn't the kind of restaurant you enjoy. And it's not as if I really need your services tonight." He winced as he realized how that last bit sounded. "Your services as a PA. What you're doing tonight isn't personal assistance. You're keeping a weird man company, and you're being gracious about it, and I appreciate it."

For a long moment, Jordan blinked at him. Then he slowly shook his head. "This isn't an imposition. I'm having fun. Okay, yeah, if it had been up to me I would have picked that pizza joint in our hotel. But then I wouldn't have had the chance to eat a mountain, would I? Besides, I can eat pizza any old time. I've never had a meal like this one. In fact—"

He stopped when the waiter appeared with the final course: a miniature mound of avocado sorbetto crowned with an aniseed cookie the size of Landry's thumbnail. A squiggle of spicy mango sauce snaked around the edge of the plate. Thankfully, the accompanying shot of espresso was standard-size.

Jordan licked the last of his dessert from his spoon. "Sometimes my mom goes on a diet, and then she eats a lot of celery because, she claims, it has negative calories. She'd love this place. You burn more calories bringing the food to your mouth than you gain from eating it."

"So if this was an eight-course meal, we'd be in danger of starving to death?"

"Exactly."

They were both quiet for the next few minutes. Jordan looked out the window, while Landry toyed with his espresso cup. Conversation elsewhere in the dining room had grown lively, and restaurant employees scurried about bearing their Lilliputian offerings. But if Landry inhaled deeply, he imagined he could catch a whiff of Jordan—chlorine and sweetness and salt. A heartier feast than anything he'd eaten.

"Can I tell you something?" Jordan said at last, his tone hesitant.

"Of course."

"I don't date much. I used to do a lot of casual hookups. Just… bars and clubs and stuff. It was fun, but I guess I outgrew it. But then… I don't know if I'm the kind of guy nobody takes seriously enough for a real relationship, or if I'm crappy at finding people who *want* a relationship. Either way, I've been pretty much flying solo. Which was good in a way, 'cause it made it easier for me to pick up and leave Seattle. But I've been hoping for more."

"You are free to—"

Quick as a snake, Jordan grabbed Landry's hand. "What I'm trying to say is that this, tonight, feels like a date. And that's a good thing. Turns out that I like hanging out with you."

Landry had a brief but fervent regret that no alcohol was at hand. He would have liked to slug down a shot or two. "I enjoy your company," he said carefully. And he didn't pull away from Jordan's grip.

"Good. I'm trying to get a feel here for how much you enjoy me. And in what specific way."

"Um…."

Jordan let go and clasped his own hands on top of the table. He looked down and chewed his lip. "God, I'm such a dork. I suck at saying important things the right way."

"Important things?"

"Yeah." Jordan looked up at Landry with wide eyes and the kind of raw, open expression that was rarer in LA than diamonds. Then his mouth stretched into a broad, warm smile that crinkled the corners of his eyes and made him more beautiful than an angel.

"Landry? I know we have separate bedrooms. But tonight I'd really like to sleep with you."

Chapter Seven

LANDRY and Jordan didn't speak on the way back to their suite. Landry had greeted Jordan's suggestion with shocked silence, and then he'd paid the ridiculous bill without a word. He didn't know what was going on in Jordan's head, although judging from his pale skin and the uneasy tension of his body, it wasn't anything good.

Landry hoped that he appeared calm and unconcerned himself. Inside, his nervous system swirled with so many emotions that he could barely keep track of them. Surprise was definitely one of them. As were trepidation, delight, caution, and his long-lost friend, lust. He simply had no idea what to say to Jordan, so he said nothing, even though he knew his silence was cruel.

Jordan didn't look at him as they crossed the casino floor and then rode the elevator up. He didn't even exclaim when they entered the suite to discover the gauze curtains closed, the lights dimmed, and the televisions playing smooth jazz. And although he marched straight into his own bedroom, he didn't pop back out to comment on the turndown service: slippers at the bedside, a bottle of water and small stack of chocolates on the nightstand.

Landry remained in the living room, paralyzed by his own inadequacies.

He was deeply relieved when Jordan reappeared a few minutes later, jacket and tie in hand. "Thanks for letting me borrow these." He held them out but avoided meeting Landry's eyes.

"You can keep them for now, until we have the chance to do some shopping and buy you more suitable clothing. Perhaps we can do that tomorrow, in fact."

Like a lamp switched on, Jordan brightened immediately. "You mean I'm not fired?"

"Of course not."

"But what I said at the restaurant—"

"Was no reason for you to lose your job." Before Jordan could respond too enthusiastically, Landry raised a warning hand. "But we do need to set some boundaries."

"Why?"

That wasn't the response Landry had expected. "Because I am your employer." That was obvious enough, wasn't it?

"Not because you're not attracted to me?"

It took a few moments for Landry to sort out the question and craft an answer. "Whether I'm attracted to you is irrelevant. I'm your—"

"My employer. Right. But it's still totally relevant." Jordan tossed the clothing onto the nearest chair and moved a step closer to Landry. "So *are* you? Attracted, I mean?"

Jesus. Landry swallowed. "I am. Of course I am. You're beautiful and charming and... vibrant."

"Good." Jordan came even nearer, close enough to settle a hand on Landry's shoulder. Close enough to converse in a soft whisper. "Because I've been wanting to kiss you since three minutes after we met, and I'd be heartbroken if you didn't feel the same way."

"I.... God, I do. But you're my employee."

"If you're worried I'm going to complain that you sexually harassed me, I'm not. Because you haven't. You're not the one who's been parading around bare-assed, and you haven't made one single inappropriate comment."

Maybe the possibility of a lawsuit had bothered Landry, who had, after all, spent a decade living with a lawyer. But that wasn't his primary reservation. He doubted Jordan was the lawsuit-slinging type. "There's a power differential. It's not fair to you."

"That would totally be true if you were pushing me for something I didn't want. But it's me pushing, and I really, really want this. Want you." His lips were so close to Landry's that Landry could almost taste them.

He felt his common sense evaporating, his resolution crumbling to dust. He clutched desperately at disappearing denials. "But if this goes wrong... your job...."

Jordan answered with a breathy chuckle that made Landry's nerves tingle. "I've lost jobs over a lot less. This is totally a risk I'm willing to take." Then he leaned in those last few inches, and they were kissing.

As kisses went, this was no barn burner. No tongues. No groping hands. Just Jordan's soft, sweet lips against Landry's—and oh God, that was more than enough. The erotic contact made Landry's long-neglected libido react like a slot machine hitting a jackpot. But not *just* erotic, the kiss also felt warm and comforting and earth-shatteringly real. The kiss was a promise to be trusted, an offer with no strings, a gift given with the purest intentions.

All that in a brief touch of skin against skin.

When they separated—although not by far—they both panted breathlessly, and Jordan smiled. "If you fire me right now, that was completely worth it."

"You're not fired."

"Good." Jordan reached up and caressed Landry's cheekbone with his thumb. "I'm glad. Kissing my boss was a gamble."

"Vegas is certainly the place for that." Landry's legs felt weak, and it took all his strength to keep his voice even and his hands to himself.

"So should I take my winnings and walk away? Or up the ante?"

Landry knew what he *wanted* Jordan to do—and what Landry wanted to do to him. It involved a lot less clothing. But he couldn't silence the voice in his head, the one that spoke in terms of appropriate employer-employee relations but was, Landry suspected, rooted in something deeper. The same voice nagged him to meet his deadlines, to plan and test and retest everything he was going to do on TV. It reminded him to dress appropriately for his position and not slouch around town in jeans and a T-shirt with his hair unstyled. It *hated* when he broke down and ate fast food.

That voice was sternly warning Landry not to get emotionally involved with Jordan.

Landry took a step back. "I'm going to take a walk."

Jordan's shoulders sagged. "Oh. Alone?"

"Yes. I need the exercise."

"Of course—you have that huge feast to work off." Although his words teased, Jordan looked disappointed and tired, which added more guilt to Landry's emotional stew.

Attempting a calm, upbeat tone, Landry said, "Feel free to enjoy the town. You can take yourself out for a real meal. Maybe you can even catch a late show somewhere— the concierge can help you find something. Use my credit card for whatever you want."

"I'm not after your money, Landry."

"I didn't mean to imply—"

But Jordan waved away the explanation and walked into his bedroom.

THE Strip was more crowded now than it had been during the day, with cars honking as they crawled down the street and throngs clogging the pavement and skywalks. Many of the people clutched oversize plastic cups of margaritas or other drinks. Some people held cell phones and shot photos or video along the way. Buskers wore superhero or showgirl costumes, or they played instruments. One rotund man wore nothing but a body thong and an Elvis mask. Another man, tall and long-haired, thrust a live snake in people's faces, eliciting many screams.

While Landry didn't enjoy being jostled among a swarm, he did appreciate his anonymity. Not a single soul called his name or demanded advice on redecorating their bathroom. He was neither Wormy from Peril nor Landry from the talk shows and magazines, but rather just another guy trying to make his way past the Venetian.

His shoes were fashionable but not ideal for walking, so by the time his wandering led him to the Wynn, his feet hurt. Despite that, he wasn't ready to return to his hotel. And to Jordan. So he limped to the Wynn's cab stand and caught a ride downtown.

While the Strip maintained some touches of glitz and glamour, the downtown Fremont Street Experience was a shining example of everything tasteless and tawdry. Literally shining, due to the bank of video screens that canopied the street and the screaming light from every storefront and casino. The buskers here were tackier, the crowds drunker, the shop trinkets chintzier. As people zoomed overhead on zip lines, Landry strongly hoped that none of them would puke as they dangled above him.

Ah, but downtown Vegas had the kind of over-the-top experiences and cheap prices that probably appealed to people from places like Peril. It was the kind of place where they could take photos to demonstrate to people back home just how wild Vegas was. And after taking their selfies, they could buy a souvenir shot glass and then duck into a casino and hope to strike it rich.

And there was also the food.

His phone dinged to inform him that several well-reviewed restaurants were nearby. He didn't go to any of them. Instead he remained on Fremont Street, searching. He bypassed the Heart Attack Grill, because even in a moment of weakness he wouldn't go that far. He finally entered a Denny's.

The last time he'd been in the franchise had been shortly after college, when money was tight and he often worked very late. Sometimes he'd visit one near his apartment, where he'd order pancakes and bacon and sort through fond memories of Ethel's Eats, Peril's only diner.

The Denny's on Fremont Street was different from his usual one in LA. For one thing, a security guard greeted him at the door. For another, this one served alcohol. And even though it was late at night, a lot of children sat in high chairs and booths. But the menu was as he remembered, and he happily ordered a meal of pancakes, hash browns, eggs, bacon, sausage, *and* ham. He asked for coffee too, and it proved to be exactly what he'd hoped for—burnt, bitter, and somewhat watery. Just like Ethel's.

He was halfway through the stack of pancakes when Jordan plopped down in the seat across from him and snagged a piece of bacon from Landry's plate.

With his fork-bearing hand frozen in midair, Landry gaped. Jordan chewed smugly.

"How?" Landry finally managed.

"Remember that app you made me download so I can track your phone if you lose it?" Double-smug.

Landry set down the fork. He was still trying to decide what to say when the waitress arrived.

Tattooed and busty, with poorly dyed hair and tired eyes, she bore little resemblance to the pompous man who'd waited on them at Le Renard Violet. But she gave Jordan a genuine smile. "Can I get something for you, honey?"

"What he's having, please. Including the coffee."

"I'll have that right on out."

After she left, Jordan reached for Landry's plate again, but Landry blocked him. "You're getting your own."

"Yeah, I know. But I'm starving."

Landry sighed and pushed his plate closer to Jordan, who took a sausage this time. He gobbled it in two bites instead of eating it salaciously, but then he winked and licked his fingers clean. Scowling,

Landry pulled the plate back and used a fork to spear the remaining sausage.

"Why are you here?" he asked after chewing and swallowing.

"Told you. Hungry."

"Jordan."

"I was hoping you'd had enough time to think and we could talk."

"In a Denny's."

"You're the one who chose this place, not me." He cocked his head. "Why *did* you choose this place? It's Vegas. Even this late, plenty of nice restaurants are open."

Landry didn't answer. Instead he poured more syrup on his pancakes and took a big bite. His head had begun to ache, probably from a combination of loud music, cigarette smoke, desert dryness, and stress. Empty calories wouldn't help, but they did give him an excuse to avoid conversation with Jordan.

Jordan was not cowed by the silence. He gazed around the restaurant for a while, then grabbed the wrapper from Landry's water straw and folded it into shapes. When that grew stale, he straightened the containers of sweeteners and jams. When the waitress delivered his food, he dug in with apparent gusto. "This could be geography too, if you squint at the plate right. The pancakes sort of look like an island. Here." He scattered a few hash browns on top of the stack. "Rocks. Or maybe fallen logs or something. Yes, this island has been cruelly deforested. It's a metaphor of environmental catastrophes. Good job, Denny's chef!"

It was hopeless. Landry wanted to be angry at Jordan for intruding, but he couldn't stop himself from snickering at this silliness.

And as soon as Jordan heard the laugh, he gave a triumphant smile. "See? You do enjoy my company."

"I never said I didn't."

"Yet you ran to the farthest reaches of chain-restaurantdom to escape me."

When Landry didn't reply, Jordan sighed theatrically. Then he brightened. "Hey! Is that Elvis eating a waffle?"

Landry twisted around to look, but all he saw was a group of drunken frat boys and a table with three middle-aged couples.

When he turned back, Jordan laughed. "Okay, no Elvis. But it was plausible, right? Please explain why you've chosen a place in which Elvis could reasonably be eating late-night breakfast."

"I was in the mood for pancakes."

"I need to tell you something, Landry." Jordan's now humorless tone made Landry's stomach clench.

"What?"

"I know about the french fries."

It sounded so absurdly like a line from a bad spy movie that Landry couldn't even place the context. "You what?"

"The french fries you ate this afternoon."

"You tracked me then too?" That came out as a squawk and made the family at the adjacent table stare.

But Jordan shook his head. "No. I just happened to be behind you when you were heading toward the hotel. I was going to call out to you, but I was curious why you were carrying a Golden Arches bag. Then I saw you eating the fries and I knew. I figured you didn't want me to know about it, so I didn't say anything."

"Until now."

Jordan spread his arms. "A little Mickey D's pales in comparison to this."

He had a good point, and by now Landry was far more embarrassed than he was angry. He also couldn't help noticing that Jordan wasn't making fun of him for his culinary choices. In fact, he'd made far more jokes at the expense of Le Renard Violet.

"Sometimes," Landry said carefully, "I need something different."

"Is it a stress-eating thing?"

"No, it's not just food. I get a craving."

"For?"

Landry struggled to find the right words. "Middle America. Every now and then, especially when I'm... emotional, I want a bit of average and mass-produced. Not gourmet and Jaguars and Dolce & Gabbana."

Jordan nodded. "McDonald's. Fords. Target."

"Yes," Landry whispered.

"Because you're still that kid from Nebraska."

"No! I mean... I don't know. I didn't belong in Peril. Some people do, and that's perfectly fine for them. Missy, my sister? She's absolutely content there. Loves her house and her neighbors, and she gets miserable if she has to visit a huge metropolis like Sidney or Grand Island. But that's not me and never was."

Jordan bit his lip thoughtfully. "I can definitely see how you'd feel more comfortable in California. But let me ask you something. All the fantastic stuff you do—the fashion, the decorating, the crafts—you enjoy it, right? You must, to be so good at it."

"I do," Landry answered sincerely. "I love it."

"Sure. But you don't have to be monogamous about it, do you? Like, I love sun *and* rain, right? Sometimes

I'm in the mood to bask, and sometimes I'd prefer to curl up inside and gaze out at the gloom."

"I don't see—"

"*You* can love that trippy fox-motif eating place *and* the home of the Grand Slam. There's nothing wrong with that."

"I didn't love Le Renard Violet," Landry admitted. "I didn't even really like it."

"You know what I mean."

Landry did, but he needed to think about it. Perhaps sensing this, Jordan quietly ate the remainder of his meal. He polished everything off, which was impressive. Landry had already abandoned the cooled remains of his eggs. But they both still had coffee, and before the waitress took their plates away, she refilled their mugs and told them to wave her down if they wanted more or were ready for the bill.

"Almost nobody knows about my cravings," Landry said at last. "Elaine does."

"She didn't mention it to me."

Good old Elaine. Landry hadn't given her enough gratitude when she worked for him.

"Steve knew too. It used to annoy him, though, so I generally only indulged after we argued."

"Why would he be annoyed?"

"It doesn't match my image. We worked so hard to create my brand, and he didn't want me to ruin it by being spotted looking frumpy in Walgreens."

Jordan caught both of Landry's hands with his own. "You're a *person*, not a brand." His brow furrowed with concern, and his mouth turned down at the corners.

"I'm... both."

Although Jordan shook his head, he didn't say anything, and he didn't let go of Landry's hands. Landry

could have pulled away easily—Jordan's grip was gentle—
but he didn't try. Like an emotional lightning rod, the
contact drew much of the turmoil away from his heart.

Eventually the waitress tended to a nearby table,
and when she turned their way, Landry smiled at her.
"Could I get the check, please?"

"Sure, honey, I'll be right on it. You two need to get
out of here and find yourself somewhere more romantic."

"See?" Jordan said after she walked away. "The
waitress thinks we make a good couple."

"She's an excellent waitress, but I'm not sure I'd
turn to her for personal advice."

"I totally would."

True to his word, Jordan grinned at her when she
returned. "Can I ask you a question without being a
pain in the ass? I know you're busy."

As Landry well knew, Jordan was too charming for
her to refuse. Some of the exhaustion lifted from her
posture, and her eyes sparkled. "Ask away, sweetheart."

"Thanks! So, this guy's my boss. But he's also
amazing, right? And we're both completely, horribly
single. So I'm trying to convince him our relationship
should get way more personal, and I'm pretty sure he's
at least a little bit into me. But he's reluctant because…
I'm not exactly sure why. Mostly because I work for
him, I guess."

Seemingly delighted by Jordan, she nodded as he
spoke. Landry had to resist the temptation to sink under
the table—or at least hide behind his hands.

"So," Jordan continued, "I bet you see a *lot* of
couples here."

"Of course I do. This is Vegas." She had dimples
when she smiled.

"Then based on your experience, do you think the two of us should be a thing? Or just employer-employee?"

She didn't answer immediately, and when she did, she addressed Landry rather than Jordan. "Honey, workers come and go. You can always find someone to work for you if you pay decently and you're not a jerk, and this guy can always find somewhere to work, I bet. But love? You better catch that when it comes close to you, 'cause you might not get a chance at it again. If you're feeling tender toward this guy—and I think you are; God knows you'd be a fool not to—then don't push him away. You'll regret it if you do."

"Thank you," Landry said, and he was sincere. He still wasn't inclined to rely on the advice of this complete stranger, but he appreciated how seriously she'd approached the task. She seemed to be genuinely trying to help, which was far more than she'd signed up for when she clocked in that day.

"Good luck, you two."

Landry left her a tip nearly as big as the bill; even without the romance counseling, she'd provided excellent service. Besides, she worked hard, and he could afford a few extra dollars. Look how much he'd wasted on their earlier ridiculous dinner.

They walked hand in hand after they left Denny's— Jordan's idea. Landry had never been prone to public displays of affection. He preferred to reserve such things for more private times. Still, it was pleasant to hold Jordan's hand. It made Landry feel less lost in the crowds.

As they walked, something aligned inside Landry. It was as if he'd long had a joint out of place, and now, strolling through the commercialized chaos with Jordan at his side, that joint slipped back where it belonged. It was a good sensation but also a big one—too big for him to analyze tonight.

Despite the late hour, the activity on Fremont Street hadn't abated, and during their Lyft ride back to the hotel, traffic remained heavy. Throngs still swarmed the casino too, and a weird sensation settled on Landry as he and Jordan walked past the card tables, as if he were trapped in an alternate dimension where time had no meaning. Except if time truly didn't exist, he wouldn't be tired, would he? Yet he yawned hugely while the elevator rose.

"Long day," Jordan agreed after echoing the yawn.

"And too much food."

"Two dinners. 'Cause the first one was maybe point two five of a meal, but Denny's made up for it."

"I agree with your calculations."

They walked slowly down the long corridor.

After entering their suite and locking the door, they stood in the entryway. Close but not quite touching.

"I need to sleep," Landry said.

"Got it. I've been pushing you really hard. Sorry."

"Maybe I need a hard push. I don't know." This time Landry reached up to trace Jordan's cheekbone. Jordan closed his eyes and breathed in as if he were basking in the sun.

Landry let his hand fall, but before he could move away, Jordan pinned him in place with an intense gaze. "Can I tell you something?" Jordan asked.

"I doubt very much I could stop you."

"Point. Look, please don't take this the wrong way. I can tell how much you loved Steve, and I bet he loved you just as much. Plus it sounds like he was fully supportive of you and your dreams, and that's hard to find in a partner. But maybe you guys got so focused on building Landry Bishop, the brand, that you neglected Landry, the man. Maybe you sort of trapped yourself inside your own packaging."

Landry had a vision of himself as a Ken doll, scrambling desperately to escape his cardboard-and-cellophane prison. But even if Ken got out, he'd still be what he was made to be, destined to do no more than sit stiffly around the Dreamhouse, smiling vacantly. Unlike Barbie, he couldn't even restyle his hair.

"I'm going to bed," Landry said.

"Okay. What do you want to do tomorrow?"

"I have work—"

"Work to do. I know. But all day?"

Impending deadlines. The *Suzee Show*. A slew of holiday-themed blog posts. Landry sighed.

But Jordan lightly touched his arm. "Tell me what I can do for you. That's what I'm here for. How can I ease your load?"

"I'll… give you a list in the morning."

"There's the spirit! And if I help you enough, will you have time to do something with me in the evening? 'Cause I have a plan."

Landry was going to simply agree and then shamble off to his room. But he found himself stepping closer, resting his palms against Jordan's jawline, and then pressing their lips together.

Still not a deep kiss, although far from chaste. Jordan's skin was a little rough from late-night stubble, his lips sweetened by pancake syrup. Wonderful. Heady enough to make Landry swoon. But he'd already processed too much that day, so he gave Jordan an additional little peck on the cheek and then walked away.

"Night," Jordan called softly.

Landry turned to look over his shoulder. "Good night, Jordan."

Chapter Eight

LANDRY had always been a morning person, so despite staying up late the night before, he awakened early. He put on his designer exercise clothes, and before leaving the suite, he succumbed to temptation and peeked in at Jordan, who'd left his door open. He had closed only the sheers over his window, so there was plenty of light to see him curled up fast asleep. He'd pulled the covers up to his neck, but one hand lay softly curved on the pillow beside his face. He looked sweet and young and vulnerable.

Landry tiptoed out of the room.

The property boasted an elaborate fitness center, mostly empty at this hour. Landry chose an elliptical machine and, after deciding the morning news made him ill, listened to his workout playlist instead. He'd originally created it as a joke—a collection of songs exclusively from the eighties. But he'd discovered that he *liked* having Madonna, Cyndi Lauper, Wham!, Olivia Newton-John, and Billy Idol as his workout buddies. And if "Eye of the Tiger" always made him imagine himself in a boxing montage, well, that could be excused.

Sweaty but pleased with himself for not letting all the Denny's calories take hold, Landry returned to the suite to discover Jordan standing in the living room in his underwear, a bottle of water in hand.

"Here," Jordan said, striding over and handing him the bottle. "Hydrate."

"But—"

"A good PA anticipates his boss's needs, right?"

Maybe Jordan had an app for stalking Landry's exercise too. But Landry could hardly complain, seeing as he was really thirsty. He downed half the bottle. "Thanks."

"How about if I get you some breakfast while you shower? Then you can compose my task list while you eat. Super efficient."

Landry couldn't argue with that. He set the bottle down and headed for the bathroom.

The hotel shower was wonderful, with excellent water pressure, endless hot water, and plenty of room to move. At home in droughty LA, Landry was very much aware of the need to conserve water, but he indulged himself this morning, luxuriating in the warmth. He sniffed the hotel-provided toiletries but opted to use his own.

By the time he emerged into the living room, dry and dressed, Jordan had arranged plates and silverware on the coffee table. "Is this all right?" he asked.

"It's perfect." And it was. A cup of fresh fruit and a slice of toast topped with braised kale and a poached egg. An enormous cup of coffee and a glass of cucumber water. Landry sat down on the couch and took a sip of coffee. "But where's yours?"

"I'll catch something later. Right now I'm on the clock. What do you want from me today?" Jordan stood with a notebook in one hand and a pen poised in the other.

Landry ate slowly, dictating as he went. Jordan should make sure to find him a good salad for lunch and keep him periodically supplied with iced tea. There were appointments to set in LA, fan emails to sort and prioritize, and a small-appliance manufacturer with questions about where to send samples they wanted Landry to review. Landry was also going to need some new outfits for hosting the *Suzee Show*, so he asked Jordan to scan ads and magazines and come up with suggestions. His blog comments needed attending to, and his Instagram account required updating. Jordan should calendar a trip to IKEA, in the interest of research for one of Landry's books. And because Landry had become dissatisfied with his pool service, he wanted Jordan to hunt for a new one. "Oh, and the Jag needs servicing. Please arrange that."

Jordan wrote everything down, asking a few pertinent questions along the way. He looked neither daunted nor upset by the length and complexity of the list. In fact, when Landry stopped talking, Jordan looked at him expectantly. "What else?"

"That should keep you busy for a while, I think. Make sure you don't neglect yourself."

"I'll be fine. Can I suggest something?"

"What?"

"They've got cabanas by the pool. How about if I book you one? Then we move you, your laptop, and your iced tea, and you can slave away outdoors. I'll make sure the room gets serviced while you're out there."

Landry opened his mouth to decline but then thought better of it. The temperature would be perfect in the shade, and he wouldn't mind a change of scenery. The hotel had one pool reserved for guests who rented the fancy suites, which meant tranquil surroundings and no screaming children. "All right."

"Really? I didn't expect you to agree so easily." Jordan cackled like a cartoon villain. "My magic is working."

"Just keep your magic from interrupting me while I'm writing."

"Done."

Jordan made a couple of quick phone calls while Landry gathered his things, and then they walked to the pool together. Jordan had arranged for the most ideally located cabana, which included a power outlet and Wi-Fi. After making sure the seat cushion was comfortable and the little table arranged perfectly, Jordan trotted over to the bar and returned minutes later with a huge glass of iced tea. "I've asked the bartender to wander by now and then to see if you need a refill. He won't bug you, though. Just ignore him if you're good. And text me if you need anything."

Landry felt like the Prince of Las Vegas. With palm trees waving in a slight breeze and sweet-scented flowers masking the chlorine scent of the pool, the entire setup was close to heaven. He liked how he could glance outside his little palace to see the hotel buildings towering around him, then turn his attention to his cozy writing nook.

True to Jordan's promise, the bartender checked in unobtrusively. Landry accomplished a lot of writing—a blog post about inexpensive accessories to dress up a holiday outfit, and one about the best culinary herbs to grow indoors over the winter. He also completed edits to a magazine article on paint color schemes for family rooms, and when he'd finished those more pleasant tasks, he brainstormed more questions for the *Suzee Show* guests. Just as he stood to stretch and have a quick break, Jordan appeared with a large paper bag and a smile. "Everything going okay?"

"Perfect," Landry said, which made Jordan brighten even more.

"Good. I come bearing mixed greens, oil and vinegar on the side, and a packet of crackers in case you're dying for carbs." As he spoke, Jordan produced the items from the bag and set them beside the laptop.

"And your morning?" asked Landry.

"Did everything except the clothing options—still working on those. Our suite has been cleaned. I had a veggie burger for lunch, and I booked you an afternoon massage at the spa, which you can totally cancel but I don't think you should."

"Massage?"

"You spend a lot of time hunched over a keyboard. It'll be good for you."

It had been ages since Landry's last massage, and honestly, it sounded wonderful. "That's a solid plan. And how about if we go shopping afterward?"

"You still want to dress me up all pretty?"

"You're pretty no matter what you wear, but you need suitable attire for certain events, and Vegas is as good a place as any to get it."

"Cool!"

Jordan left Landry to work some more. Perhaps fueled by the promise of the spa and shopping, the words flowed easily onto the screen. So much so that Landry packed up a little early, lugged his laptop to the suite, and texted Jordan. *Heading for the spa shortly. Did you book yourself a massage too?*

Jordan replied immediately. *I'm not good with massages. Too wiggly. Also kinda ticklish.*

And there went Landry's brain again, romping happily through X-rated pastures. "Stop it!" he scolded himself. *How about a fancy shave instead?*

I've never had anyone shave me. Is it weird?

I think you'll like it. Meet me there. Landry followed up with a call to the salon and was relieved to find that they'd be able to accommodate Jordan.

They arrived at the same time, each from a different direction. And dammit, as soon as Landry saw him, his heart raced and his skin tingled. He felt as if he'd been injected with the best kind of drug, a chemical equivalent of rose-colored glasses, leaving his head clear but softening the world's cruel edges.

"Fancy shave?" Jordan asked Landry as he entered the spa.

"With a facial."

Jordan covered his mouth and snorted with amusement, the world's oldest twelve-year-old, and although Landry rolled his eyes, he was secretly charmed.

They went to separate areas for their treatments. Landry's masseuse was excellent. She made him groan with mingled pain and pleasure.

"Your shoulders are really tight." She said it three or four times, shaking her head with wonder. And then she dug in deeper, until he was certain she'd squished all his muscles to goo.

He walked out of the treatment room feeling slightly sore but also loose and unexpectedly mellow.

His masseuse made him drink a big bottle of water spiked with an assortment of fruits and herbs. "Finish it off," she ordered. "You need to detox from everything that I released from your muscles." Although Landry was skeptical of the scientific basis of this, he obeyed. The water tasted good.

But when Jordan emerged a few minutes later… oh my. His skin glowed, and the barber had obviously given in to the temptation to play with that beautiful hair. The short ponytail was now gone, and what remained was styled casually but artfully. Picking up on Landry's hungry stare, Jordan gave a wolfish grin.

"I like weird shaves with facials," he announced in the elevator.

"And the massage worked miracles. Thanks for thinking of it. In fact, when we get back home, I'd like you to arrange for someone to come weekly to the house." Maybe with regular rubs, his shoulders would lose some tightness.

Jordan made a note in his book.

Back in their suite, Jordan waited while Landry showered again, washing away the remnants of the massage oil. When he came back into the living room, Jordan was peering intently at an iPad. "Looking at potential *Suzee Show* outfits," he explained. "I don't know if I'm on the right track, though. I don't have anything like your sense of style."

"I wasn't born with it, and I certainly didn't pick it up in Peril."

"Your hometown isn't a fashion mecca?"

Landry snorted. "There was one shop downtown that sold women's and kids' clothing. The menswear store went out of business when I was in grade school. Other than that, you bought your clothing at Svoboda Ranch and Home, you mail-ordered it, or you drove somewhere else."

"I bet you'd look adorable in overalls and a John Deere baseball cap."

Landry glared and vowed never to let Jordan know that a photo once existed of him wearing exactly that. Landry had been only three years old at the time, and therefore generally unable to voice his sartorial preferences, but still. That picture had been hanging on his parents' wall when Landry moved to California. If he was lucky, Missy had thrown it out after their mother died.

"What we did have, even in Peril, were magazines. I read many of them and paid close attention. *That*'s how I learned to dress."

"Maybe. But your... panache is innate. I bet I could plunk you down in overalls in the middle of a cornfield and you'd still manage to look chic." Jordan's words were complimentary, but his tone and expression bore real fervor—the marks of a true believer.

Dammit, Landry was blushing. "Corn isn't grown in the Sandhills," he muttered.

"What do they grow there?"

"Cattle."

Jordan laughed. "So can I picture you in chaps and a Stetson instead?"

"Don't you dare." Landry sighed. "Let's go find something suitable for you to wear."

Landry had decided to get Jordan a few solid base pieces, the kinds of trousers and jackets that might suit a variety of situations, and to spice them up with a selection of shirts and accessories. The mall adjacent to the hotel was perfect for this purpose since it contained several high-end boutiques. Jordan followed along obediently, his face reflecting its usual expression of expectant happiness. On anyone else, Landry would have found that mien irritating. He didn't like perky. But on Jordan he found it endearing.

Shit.

He chose the shop carefully, a designer whose styles were youthful without being overly trendy. There were no other customers, and the salesman—who looked like Ricky Martin's sexy younger brother—rushed over. "Oh my God! Landry Bishop! I'm so sorry. I know I shouldn't be gushing, but I am a huge fan."

"Thank you. That's very kind." After years of practice, Landry had become fairly adept at handling public admiration, but it still made him uncomfortable. It was hard to pull off graciousness and humility without being awkward. "This is my PA, Jordan. We're looking for a few foundation pieces for him."

The salesman clapped his hands as if this was the best news he'd heard in months. And maybe it was; he probably worked largely on commission. "Terrific! I'm Emilio, and I'd be thrilled to help you."

Landry and Emilio spent a long time perusing the store's offerings, rejecting most options but choosing several. Although Jordan occasionally chipped in with an opinion or preference, mostly he waited good-naturedly, watching passersby through the store windows. Eventually Landry was satisfied with the selections.

"Let me get the dressing room set up," Emilio said. "Be right back."

As soon as Emilio was out of earshot, Jordan sidled close to Landry and spoke in a whisper. "See those sweatpants over there? They're eight hundred bucks! Who pays that kind of money for sweatpants?"

"Don't worry about it. We're not buying you casual clothing."

"But if the sweats are that much—and Jesus, that T-shirt is four hundred!—how much is that suit Emilio plucked off the rack?"

"Considerably more," Landry admitted. "But I'm paying, not you. It's like providing my employee a work uniform."

"But… Christ, Landry. It's a lot of dough to throw around. Can't you make me look good cheaper?"

"You always look good. But my PA is part of my brand. You make an impression when you're in public, and we need to make sure it's the right impression."

"Yeah, okay. I get it."

Emilio came back, and it was Landry's turn to wait while Emilio helped Jordan try things on.

Jordan emerged in a closely tailored navy blue suit with a cut that emphasized his broad shoulders, slim hips, and long legs. Landry almost forgot to breathe.

"He looks like a model," said Emilio, who seemed as stunned as Landry.

Jordan glanced down at himself. "It's a nice suit."

"We're getting that one." It was the easiest decision Landry had made in a long time.

They also bought two pairs of somewhat more casual trousers and a blazer that went with both. Emilio was ecstatic. Landry signed an autograph for him and promised him tickets to the *Suzee Show* the next time Emilio was in LA. "Just email me in advance." Jordan, meanwhile, grumbled under his breath that the bill would have covered several months of his Seattle rent.

But the shopping excursion wasn't complete. They visited other stores to buy shirts, a couple of sweaters, ties, a lightweight jacket for what passed as winter in

LA, and a pair of shoes—all to be delivered to their suite. Aside from occasional exclamations about the prices, Jordan was a remarkably good sport.

"I feel like I'm ten again," he said as a saleswoman held a red cashmere V-neck against his chest. "Every August Mom would drag me to the mall to buy me new clothes."

"Did you hate it?"

"Eh. I got bored, but it was also nice to spend time with her. She's a really cool lady, even if she is my mother. Plus she bribed me with lunch in the food court. I can be bought for Hot Dog on a Stick." He waggled his eyebrows suggestively, making the saleswoman giggle.

Eventually satisfied that they'd bought enough, Landry led them back toward the hotel. "Thank you," he said to Jordan as they exited the mall.

"What are you thanking me for? You're the one who just spent a small country's GDP on making me look presentable."

"Thank you for letting me do this. I know it wouldn't be your preference."

"If I made a list of the top one hundred crappy things I've had to do to earn a living, this wouldn't be on it."

Someday Landry would ask him for that list. He wanted to know more about Jordan's past, about the combination of circumstances that had brought this incredible man to his doorstep.

Jordan bumped his shoulder lightly against Landry's. "All those salespeople recognized you."

That was true. Not all of them had enthused as openly as Emilio, but they had all appeared happy to have him as a customer. And he'd signed autographs and taken selfies with every one of them.

"In their line of work, I suppose they've encountered me now and then."

"Hmm. But I kinda see what you mean about the brand. I mean, if some random shoe salesman in Nevada has expectations of you, well, it's hard for you to keep a low profile."

"It's what I signed up for." Landry was never going to complain about the price of fame, not when he'd worked so hard to get it. Yes, there were downsides. But as Jordan had just pointed out, every job brought challenges, and Landry wasn't going to whine about having to keep up his image when millions of people mopped floors or flipped burgers for minimum wage.

They crossed the casino floor, navigating around people with suitcases, people pushing tiny dogs in strollers, people texting, and people meandering with cigarettes in hand. Conversation would have been difficult, so neither said anything until they were alone in the elevator.

"It's really hard on you sometimes, isn't it?" asked Jordan.

"What?"

"Being the official version of yourself."

Landry shrugged.

The elevator opened on their floor, and they walked down the corridor. But right after they closed the suite's door behind them, Jordan put a hand on Landry's arm. "Elaine used to help you out with this, right? Help you do some of the stuff you want to do but have to be sneaky about?"

"Yes." She made fast-food runs on his behalf and rescheduled meetings so he could binge-watch *Supernatural* and *Friends*, and she'd pretended not to notice when he spent the morning working in his office—unshowered, unshaven—wearing ratty old Bermuda shorts and a T-shirt.

He hadn't needed this kind of help from her often, but he'd appreciated it.

Jordan bounced on his toes again. "That's what I'm gonna do too, then. It'll be an official part of my job description."

It was funny. Such a simple thing, yet Landry felt as if Jordan had suddenly lifted a great weight from his shoulders. "Thank you."

"Can we start with tonight? Will you let me give you a fun evening that has nothing to do with your brand?"

Landry had reservations, but he couldn't refuse Jordan when he looked so eager. "Fine."

Jordan whooped his delight.

Chapter Nine

"**TELL** me you're kidding."

"Nope. Dead serious." Jordan leaned forward and handed a tip to the driver, then hopped out of the car holding Landry's hand and dragged him out as well.

"But it's a sex museum."

Jordan tugged him toward the door. "We're not here for the museum."

The night had begun tamely enough, even though Jordan had appeared slightly disappointed Landry hadn't packed any jeans. He seemed somewhat assuaged when Landry agreed to wear Jordan's long-sleeved V-neck tee. It actually gave Landry a strange little thrill to wear something that had spent so many hours in close contact with Jordan's skin. The shirt was clean, of course, but Landry imagined it still carried a bit of Jordan's scent.

Once dressed, they took the hotel monorail to the Luxor, where they ate hot dogs at the food court. Then they walked back up the Strip, stopping for frozen yogurt along the way. Landry dripped a bit of it onto his chest. Laughing, Jordan wiped it off with his fingertip and then licked the finger clean, much to the amusement of the teenagers nearby.

Jordan had remained stubbornly silent about their next destination. He'd even made Landry stand at a distance so as not to overhear what Jordan whispered to the driver. And now here they were, at a sex museum.

Once inside, Jordan had a brief discussion about show tickets with the woman at the counter. Ah. The museum had a theater. And apparently Jordan had bought them second-row seats.

"*Puppetry of the Penis*?" Landry asked as they sat on folding chairs in the small auditorium. "What does that mean?"

"Pretty much as advertised."

The opener was a stand-up comedian who did a short set. She was funny, Landry had to admit, but he remained worried about the main act.

And then two naked men walked onstage and began to create various shapes with their cocks and balls. Sombreros. Snails. Hamburgers. It was really silly, and Landry laughed so hard that his eyes teared. Even better was having Jordan sitting so close by, laughing right with him.

Steve would have been appalled by the show. But Steve was gone, and Landry was having a wonderful time. *I love you, Stevie. But Jordan has become important to me.*

After the show, the performers came out—fully clothed—to sign books. Jordan, of course, insisted on buying one. Then he called for a car to pick them up.

"Horrible?" Jordan asked as they waited outside.

"Unexpected. But nowhere near my list of one hundred horrible things I've had to do."

Jordan laughed and gave him a one-armed hug.

"What made you choose this?" asked Landry. Had Jordan thought the show would shock him? God, did Landry come off as a prude?

"You said you'd already seen all the big shows, and I thought it would be fun."

That simple. "You know, you've already secured the job. You're a wonderful PA. You don't have to go to this much effort to stay employed."

"Two things. One, I *like* to put in effort and do my job well. I said when you interviewed me: I like to make people happy. It makes me feel useful. And two, I didn't plan tonight so I can keep my job. I did it for you. 'Cause I specifically want to make *you* happy."

Almost everyone else was already gone, leaving them alone in the parking lot. Across the freeway, the big hotels glowed proudly. But on this side, despite the nearby strip joints, their particular corner was quiet.

"Why me, Jordan? I see why you'd want the job, but not why you'd risk it. You can go to any gay bar in LA and instantly pick up dozens of men better-looking than me."

"It's not about looks. You're sexy, no doubt about it, but that's not the thing."

"The thing. What *is* the thing?" Plaintive, because Landry didn't understand. He knew fashion, food, entertaining, décor. He had a fairly solid handle on the industry. He could pen a decent blog post or appear on TV without making a fool of himself. But for the life of him, he couldn't fathom Jordan's motivations.

Jordan didn't answer immediately; he stared at an advertising poster on the museum's exterior wall. Then he turned to Landry. "My parents met in a dentist's waiting room. Just two chatty strangers waiting for fluoride treatments. He's a radio news reporter, and she's a nurse. Seven days later, they got married. Everyone they knew—*everyone*—told them they were making a huge mistake. But Mom says that five minutes after they started talking, *click*, everything fit together just right. And Dad says he knew before their first date that he was already in love with her. Maybe you don't believe in love at first sight, Landry. But they've been married almost forty years now."

"That's a really sweet story."

"Yep, and I've heard it approximately eighty billion times. Ugh, and they still kiss in front of me. And hold hands, and cuddle on the couch."

Landry couldn't help but smile. "Sounds horrifying."

"It is! Okay, and here's the thing, and it might freak you out. Probably will." He took a deep breath. "I've felt that *click* too. For the first time in my life. With you. And it wasn't, *Oh, he gave me this cool job*, or even *Wow, this guy is hot*. It was… *Landry Bishop fits me*. Like that great suit you bought me today. Just *click*, and I knew for sure, that first time I made you breakfast. And you're gonna ask how I could possibly know that when I didn't even know *you*, but I did. Fate. Karma. Chemistry. I dunno. But it's real." He grabbed Landry's hands and held tight.

"Oh." That was all Landry could manage. Once again, he had no handle on his own thoughts and emotions.

"Freaked-out?"

"Maybe. Yes."

"Sorry."

"Don't be. I asked; you were honest."

Jordan cocked his head. "Did you feel that click with Steve?"

"No. I felt a big wallop of lust. His office, remember?"

"Right," Jordan said with a chuckle.

"That initial rush subsided. It never went away completely, but Stevie and I...." Landry tried for an analogy that made sense. "You know that armchair in my living room?"

"The one you sit in when you take a few minutes to watch TV. Sure."

"Pairing up with Steve was like settling into that chair. It's a very good piece of furniture—really well crafted. I can trust it to support me completely. The chair makes me feel good." He sighed. Poor Stevie deserved more than becoming a metaphorical seat. "I'm not exactly sure what his take on the matter was. I think he liked supporting."

Jordan's eyes gleamed in the parking lot lights. "And how do you feel about me?"

"Attracted. Confused. Conflicted."

"No click?" Jordan asked sadly.

"I feel more contented, I know that. Somewhat better… aligned. I'm not sure that I'd recognize a click if I felt it."

Their car rolled up to the curb. They climbed into the wide back seat and sat, silent, not touching. Splashes of color from the neon lights washed across them as they rode.

They took the elevator up to their suite, where that same soft jazz played on the TV screens and the housekeeper had neatened the little stacks of magazines. Landry thanked Jordan very sincerely for a good evening. Jordan promised to tackle a new list of chores in the morning.

Landry washed up in his overlarge bathroom, took off his shoes and socks and trousers, and climbed into bed. He used the tablet to douse the lights.

He still wore Jordan's T-shirt. Jordan hadn't asked for it back. It had probably cost twenty bucks at a big-box store. Soft, slightly frayed at the cuffs. Comfortable. Uncharacteristically, Landry fell asleep almost at once.

He dreamed he was at the *Suzee Show*, but instead of standing onstage, he sat in the audience. Strangers filled the other seats, all of them gazing raptly forward at Suzee, who was interviewing one of the penis puppetry performers. The guy wore nothing but tennis shoes. He and Suzee were talking about who might win next year's Golden Globes.

Then suddenly the man disappeared and Suzee stood at the edge of the stage. "Time for prizes, people!"

The audience cheered. So did Landry, because he wanted a prize very badly. Not Portuguese napkins, though. He already owned those. Slot machines popped out of the floor in front of each seat. They were smaller than the ones in Vegas but just as sparkly, each with a different theme. Landry's theme was the Midwest, and the face of the machine bore cartoon images of corn and soybeans, pigs and cattle, and an old-fashioned windmill like the ones that still graced some Nebraska farms.

"Take your chances!" Suzee shouted.

Landry pulled the lever. The reels spun, at first too quickly for the symbols to be visible, and then more slowly. Instead of traditional things like cherries or sevens, the reels showed chairs and items of clothing. But when the reels stopped entirely, Landry couldn't make out the symbols at the pay line; everything was too blurry.

"Will you take this payout or try again?" That was Suzee, and she must have been addressing him, because the rest of the audience had disappeared.

"I don't know what the payout is!"

She gave him a shinier, showbizzier smile than the real Suzee ever would. "Take your chances, Wormy." Music started blaring, and Landry recognized it as the tune that ended the *Suzee Show*. The stage lights switched off.

"Fine!" Landry desperately shouted. "I'll stand!" Even in the dream he knew the term applied to cards, not slots, but it seemed especially apt when his seat began to quake, forcing him to leap to his feet.

Jordan crawled out from under the chair. He wore overalls and nothing else. "Congratulations, Landry! I'm all yours. And all you have to do to keep me is be someone else entirely!"

Landry awoke with a start, his heart racing. "I don't even know if that was a nightmare," he whispered. He didn't seem to know much of anything about his inner self anymore. With a sharp pang, he realized that one of the things he missed about Steve was advice. Whenever Landry had faced a quandary, Steve had immediately set aside whatever he was working on so he could listen carefully to Landry's situation. Then he gave balanced and well-reasoned suggestions. Until now, Landry hadn't recognized how heavily he'd relied on Steve's counsel.

Who could he turn to now?

Glancing at the bedside tablet—which also served as a clock—Landry saw it wasn't as late as he'd assumed. He must have tumbled into that dream very quickly. And since it was barely past midnight in Nevada, it wouldn't be rude to text someone just after ten in Hawaii.

With mixed relief and guilt, he reached for his phone.

Can we talk?

He waited three eternities for Elaine to text back, and then he breathed a huge sigh at her response. *Sure. Call me.*

He considered FaceTiming her, but he knew his hair must resemble a fright wig. Also, she'd notice the shirt he was wearing, and she'd know it wasn't his— that would just complicate things further. He opted for a regular phone call.

"Am I interrupting something?" he asked.

"Nope. I'm in the middle of a hard session of lanai-sitting."

"Mai tai in hand?"

She laughed. "Not tonight. Mom and Dad went out to play mah-jongg and turned in as soon as they got home. I'm feeling naturally relaxed, alcohol not needed. But what's wrong and why are you whispering?"

Damn. Of *course* she'd notice that. "I don't want him to hear me."

"Who? Are you being held hostage in a car trunk? 'Cause then you should've called 911 instead of me."

"Hilarious. I'm in a hotel suite in Las Vegas. Jordan's in the room next door."

"*Is* he now?"

"What's that supposed to mean?"

"Landry, what's your crisis?"

"Augh." He flopped back against the pillows. "I'm not even sure. My head's a mess."

"I always thought you were relatively sane for a guy who lives in LA. You don't go around telling everyone that vaccines are part of a conspiracy between extraterrestrials and the Illuminati, and you're not wearing anyone's placenta as jewelry."

Her words comforted him, mostly because he knew plenty of people who did those things. Compared to that, angsting over his love life was incredibly normal. "Thank you. You've helped already."

"What other precious drops of wisdom can I bestow?"

"I don't…. I can't even explain this." He thumped his forehead a few times with the heel of his free hand. It didn't help. "Jordan."

"He's not working out for you?"

"No, he's great. He picks things up really quickly, and he's completely dedicated to me."

"That doesn't really sound like a problem."

Landry dropped his voice even more. "He's *too* dedicated."

"Meaning?"

"He has this theory about people clicking—"

"Oh, yeah. His parents. It's part of the official family lore."

Relieved he didn't have to explain, Landry nodded in the darkness. "He thinks he's clicked with me."

"Is that what the kids are calling it nowadays?"

"Elaine!" He remembered he was supposed to be whispering. "We haven't um…."

"Enjoyed the benefits of physical congress? I get it, Lord Thistlebottom."

He could have mentioned the kisses, but they weren't really the point. "I don't know what to do about this."

"Are you into him?"

"I… yes. God, yes. He's like… like digging through a pile of thrift shop knickknacks and discovering an original Henry Moore. Like biting into a dumpling and discovering it's filled with perfectly spiced meat. Like—"

"Got it. You're into him."

Landry let out a long breath. "Yeah."

"Again, doesn't sound like a problem. You're both single. And he really is a good kid."

"I'm his boss."

"Uh-huh. And does that aspect bug him?"

"No," Landry admitted. "He promised not to sue. But I guess that's not the real issue anyway. I just…. I don't know." Great. Whining was going to solve everything.

"Did you ever take any psych classes?"

"I majored in design. We covered the psychology of color."

"Then no. I *did* take psych classes—real ones. And one thing I learned is that nobody can be in a healthy relationship until he feels comfortable with who he is by himself."

That made perfect sense. If you were planning a meal, you couldn't choose the right side dishes if you hadn't decided on a main course. But it didn't apply to him. "I was in a healthy relationship, remember?"

She paused before answering. "You were practically a baby when you and Steve met. Your relationship worked really well for the Landry you were then. But what about now? Do you really know who you are? Who you want to be?"

"No," Landry whimpered. "So I should stay away from Jordan until I'm done with my pre-midlife crisis? Oh my God… I'm hurtling toward midlife. I think I'm going to have a panic attack."

"Focus, Landry. Breathe. What you do with Jordan is up to you. I wouldn't recommend the two of you running off to the chapel tomorrow and getting hitched by Elvis, but that doesn't mean you need to wear hazmat suits around each other. Try out being friends.

Maybe even try out being lovers. Just try to make sure neither of you gets hurt."

"You make it sound so easy."

"That's my job—making things easier for you. Even still."

It felt good to smile. "You're the best."

They spent some time after that chatting about a great beach she'd discovered that week and how she'd been doing aqua aerobics classes. She and her parents were considering repainting the kitchen, so Landry pledged his input if she sent him some photos. He told her about the penis puppets. She laughed herself into a snorting fit.

"Thanks, Elaine. For being there."

"I'll always be here for you, Landry. Even when I'm far away."

Chapter Ten

LANDRY set down his phone and used the tablet to open the blackout curtains. Unfortunately, the lights from the Strip weren't enough to keep him from tripping over the slippers left by the turndown service. He recovered without damaging hotel property or incurring bodily injury, made his way to the window, and gazed down at the spectacle.

Simon and Garfunkel had sung about neon gods, but he saw nothing divine in the garish signs. The Strip was one long facade—a veneer of easy wealth, easy sex, easy entertainment. He was getting tired of veneers.

"Can't sleep?"

Landry spun around and discovered Jordan in the doorway, wearing nothing but boxer briefs with an image of Darth Vader. The shadows and colored lights played off his bare skin, giving him an ethereal air. He was so beautiful, and nothing about him was a facade.

"I was asleep," Landry said. "Woke up. You?"

"I was kinda tossing and turning. I don't think I got enough exercise today."

"I kept you too tied up. Make sure you take a break tomorrow to use the fitness center."

"I wouldn't mind if you tied me up." The wide grin sent shivers of want down Landry's spine.

When Jordan continued to linger in the doorway, Landry waved him over. They stood side by side at the window.

"Everything out there looks so far away," Jordan said. "Like it's not even real."

"Like a movie set."

"Yeah. When I was a kid, sometimes we'd fly to Philly to visit my grandparents. I used to look out the airplane window and pretend the landscape was a toy. Like a giant Lego set or something. I'd think about how I wanted to rearrange stuff. How about you?"

Landry shook his head. "The first time I flew, I was eighteen and on my way to college. And I was scared to death. I was certain California was going to eat me alive. I thought every person I met would take one look at me and think, *Oh, that's just Wormy Bishop from Peril. What a hayseed.*"

"Wormy?"

Oops. He hadn't meant to let that secret slip. "Childhood nickname. Bookworm. Because I spent more time in the library than playing football with my cousins."

"If it makes you feel any better, I was Beaver Boy—until I got braces and my face caught up to my teeth."

Landry chuckled. It *did* make him feel better. "You have very nice teeth."

"I'll let my orthodontist know." Jordan moved an inch or two closer. "If leaving Peril was so scary, how come you did it?"

"I had to."

"Law on your heels?"

Although Landry wasn't looking at him, he heard the smile in Jordan's voice.

"I'm fairly certain I avoided the Most Wanted list." He set a palm against the cool glass. "Living in Peril was like always wearing somebody else's clothing— somebody with completely different tastes and sizes. Nobody was awful to me there. But it didn't fit me."

He would sit in the bleachers during high school football games, or in a booth at the local Dairy Queen, or in a pew at church, and feel like a movie extra who'd been badly miscast. Everybody played along as if they didn't notice that he didn't belong there, but *he* noticed. Always. And it wasn't just because he was gay, although that didn't help. A boy who stockpiled issues of *Martha Stewart Living* and fantasized about owning a La Cornue range was never going to be truly happy in a town where folks tended toward John Deere baseball caps and wagon wheels décor.

Jordan's question came quietly. "And LA *does* fit you?"

Landry didn't answer.

Down below, cars still trolled the street and vacationers marched up and down the sidewalks in search of their next drink, their next sure bet. But Landry's room was quiet and cozy, and Jordan stood so very close. Landry had seen him several times wearing less than he was now—once wearing nothing at all—

but window glass and yards of concrete had usually separated them. No barriers stood between them now except for Landry's own hesitancy.

He took a small step sideways and wrapped his arm around Jordan's waist. He could have happily remained like that for a long time, even though the long sleeve on the T-shirt meant he couldn't feel Jordan's bare skin. Landry's hand sat comfortably on Jordan's Vader-clad hip.

Jordan sighed like an exhausted worker finally getting into a warm bed. He mirrored Landry's movement, draping an arm around Landry's waist, and then tilted his head to rest in the crook of Landry's neck.

It was the last part that undid Landry.

Lots of people hugged or kissed him—people did that in Hollywood all the time. But the world contained over seven billion human beings, and exactly one of them could lean against him and make him feel so perfectly in place.

Was that a *click*? He had no idea. Even if it wasn't, the feeling was far too important to ignore.

Landry kissed Jordan's hair, which still smelled of product from the hotel salon. Then he kissed again, squeezed Jordan just a little more tightly, and rubbed his cheek along the crown of Jordan's head.

Jordan tightened his grip too, and he made a deep, happy sound somewhere between a moan and a purr. He squiggled around to face Landry, which allowed each of them a fuller embrace. Nose to nose, hips to hips, their mingled breaths coming a little faster, their lips millimeters apart.

"Do you know something I like about you, Landry?"

"My ass?" It was a natural response, considering Jordan's hands had migrated there and were kneading gently at Landry's glutes.

"It's a very nice ass, yes, but I was going for deeper qualities. I love how you work so hard to make things more perfect—prettier, tastier, better themed. And I love how you have a solid core of integrity."

Landry chose to ignore the use of *love*. The word terrified him. "That's two things."

"Consider one a bonus compliment. How have you stayed so grounded even though you're famous?"

"A minor celebrity at best. And… I don't know." *You can take the boy out of Nebraska, but you'll never take all the Nebraska out of the boy.* "So do I get to compliment *you* now?"

"Please do."

"You're special. A jewel."

Jordan laughed so softly that Landry felt it more than heard it. "Nobody's called me that before. Usually I'm more of a flake."

"Anyone who labels you a flake isn't paying attention. When you focus on something, you give yourself a hundred percent to the effort."

Jordan responded by giving himself a hundred percent to kissing Landry.

This kiss wasn't a sweet brushing of lips. It was deep and needy, with both Landry and Jordan gasping and groaning, clutching each other's ass, tangling tongues. He felt Jordan's pulse pounding with his own, and even through closed eyes, Landry saw sparkling lights. Something inside him released—not a click but a *pop*, as if something had just snapped into place. Not just a joint realignment, but a fundamental sense of rightness and completeness.

Suddenly filled with urgency and tight, hot *want*, Landry pulled Jordan forward. Jordan tripped on those damn slippers, but Landry kept him from falling. And then Jordan *was* falling, but gently, landing on the mattress with Landry on top of him.

Years ago Landry had helped a pop music star plan a retro luau in her backyard. Everything had gone smoothly—pupu platters ready for serving, Don Ho blasting from the speakers, rum drinks poured into tiki cups with pineapple and maraschino cherries speared on plastic swords. The hostess had looked darling in a grass skirt and floral bikini top. Then her dolt of a boyfriend, deciding the fire in the pit wasn't big enough, poured lighter fluid onto the flames.

Whoosh! Luckily there had been no casualties.

Landry thought of that *whoosh*—of glowing embers turning suddenly into a roaring inferno—as he writhed on top of Jordan's warm body, groping what he could reach and kissing Jordan's mouth and neck and shoulders. Jordan was kissing and licking too, and Landry was being consumed. But damn, he was going to revel in every moment until he burned to ashes.

Landry's shirt came off. Magically—just a few tugs and it somehow disappeared. Landry's Calvin Klein underwear dematerialized next, followed closely by Darth Vader. That left nothing but skin against glorious skin, and Jordan and Landry did their best to maximize that contact.

Landry hadn't brought condoms or lube, since he hadn't expected to need them. If Jordan happened to be more prescient or better prepared, Landry didn't want to wait for a run to Jordan's bathroom. Anyway, they didn't need supplies tonight; fingers and tongues sufficed. They stroked here and there, sucked and nibbled on exquisitely sensitive bits of flesh, rocked against each other as their sweat united them in sticky, sex-scented splendor. The flashing lights from the Strip lit up the room like a silent fireworks show.

Jordan mumbled "amazing," or something like that—Landry's pulse pounded so loudly he had trouble hearing. He moved to his knees, straddling Jordan's waist, and gazed down at him in wonder.

Then Jordan gently scraped his teeth across Landry's nipple as his fingertips teased the cleft of Landry's ass, and Landry's body zinged with marvelous electricity. "Fuck yes!" he shouted, slamming his hands against the headboard, not caring whether someone might hear. Another delightful movement of Jordan's fingers and Landry's leg jerked sideways of its own accord, granting Jordan better access and also knocking something noisily off the nightstand. "Yes!" he repeated before bending down to suck greedily at the crook of Jordan's neck.

Everything was heat and friction and taste, and nothing in the history of the universe had ever been this good.

But still Landry wanted more. With his lips still pressed to Jordan's sweet-salty skin, Landry sprawled on top of him, aligning their cocks together. Jordan moaned and moved his fingers a bit deeper—not quite inside Landry's body, but close enough to make Landry buck and thrust and growl as Jordan drove his own hips upward.

"God, L-lan!" As Jordan gasped these words, the wet heat of his climax proved exactly enough to pull Landry over the edge as well. Even then, they weren't finished. Still shuddering with aftershocks and heedless of the mess at their groins, they kissed some more, Landry carding fingers through Jordan's damp hair.

"Sleep in my bed?" Landry asked when he'd caught his breath. Because that was what he wanted now, maybe even more than he'd wanted sex.

Jordan gently cupped Landry's cheek. "Every night until you kick me out."

Chapter Eleven

MORNING sex was a new thing for Landry, but Jordan's contagious enthusiasm caused them both to go at it with more vigor than Landry would have thought possible. Afterward they sprawled on the mattress, bathed in the afterglow.

"I should go exercise," said Landry.

"I thought we just did."

"Cardio, yes. But today is supposed to be a leg day."

Jordan laughed and stroked Landry's flank. "They're great legs."

They ended up going to the fitness center together. And although Landry had expected some awkwardness—perhaps a shadow of regret on Jordan's part—the opposite proved to be true. Jordan was cheerier than ever, and their interactions felt as smooth and easy as if they'd been working together forever. Back in their suite, they paired up in the oversize shower, and afterward Jordan watched Landry's skin and hair regime with fascination. "You know, you'd look just as good without the creams and goos."

"Perhaps, but I'm accustomed to using them."

"Sure, Lord Thistlebottom."

Landry gave Jordan's butt a satisfying swat.

Later, Landry again dictated a list of tasks, and Jordan took notes as assiduously as before. But this time Jordan kissed Landry's forehead when the list was complete. "Don't work too hard, okay? Do you want a cabana?"

"No… but maybe we could find a quiet corner somewhere else?"

They settled on a lounge reserved for the fancy-suite guests, which included comfortable seating, light foot traffic, and an array of snacks and cold drinks. If anyone had consulted Landry, he would have told them the room's color scheme was slightly dated. New carpeting and wallpaper might be too much, but at least the abstract paintings could be changed. None of it distracted him from work, though. Jordan mostly left him alone, although he periodically texted a quick question.

Shortly after noon he arrived with a lovely salad. "Three kinds of dressing," he announced, setting little plastic cups on the table in front of Landry. "'Cause I wasn't sure which you'd want. Those cubes among the greens are spiced tofu. I figured you might want some protein but nothing too heavy after last night."

"It was a good night."

Jordan's answering smile was a nine on the Jordan Stryker Scale, which Landry had just invented as a rubric for measuring Jordan's apparent happiness. "It really, totally was."

"When we get home—"

Smile disappearing, Jordan sat close beside him and spoke quietly. "This isn't a stays-in-Vegas thing, is it?"

"What?"

"You know—what happens in Vegas...."

It took Landry a moment to decipher the meaning, and when he did, his chest ached. He took Jordan's hand in both of his. "If you're asking whether I intended this as a temporary vacation... fling, no. That wouldn't be fair to you. And it's not what I want."

"Me either."

Landry nodded. "What I was going to say was, when we return home, I'm going to have to spend a lot less time playing and more time buckling down."

That made Jordan's eyebrows rise, but he didn't say anything. He had folded his lips between his teeth as if he were literally biting back words. He gently withdrew his hand and fussed over Landry's lunch, setting out a paper napkin and plastic utensils and carefully unsnapping the lid off the salad. Then he stood. "Anything else you need right now? Iced tea?"

Landry pointed to the bottle of water next to his laptop. "I'm set, thanks. Feel free to relax when your work's done, but meet me in the suite at six thirty."

"Sure."

Taking a few bites of his salad now and then, Landry finished a reasonable amount of writing throughout the afternoon. He outlined two book chapters and finished a blog entry on makeup storage hacks. Then he threw away the trash and packed up everything else before heading back to his room. He had a long phone conversation with Suzee's producer, followed by shorter calls to a few people he hoped would supply promo items for the show. Even if a demo fell flat or an interview proved tedious, he could keep the audience loyal by giving them freebies. He happily scored several good items, including a hairbrush claiming to be tangle-proof, a faux fur throw blanket, and a set of noise-canceling headphones. He'd need to keep working on this project, but it was a good start. Actually, he was pleasantly surprised to accomplish anything at all, considering his mind kept wandering to thoughts of Jordan. Sense memories of Jordan.

He'd just finished finagling gel socks that were supposed to improve dry skin when Jordan walked into the suite, plastic bag in hand.

"You did some shopping?" Landry asked.

"A little."

"What did you get?" Landry couldn't make out the logo on the bag. Not that it was any of his business.

"Oh, nothing. This and that. But what should I wear for dinner tonight?"

Ignoring the obvious change of subject, Landry led him to the closet and helped him choose an outfit. Truthfully, Jordan needed only a little guidance this time. Once dressed, he followed Landry to *his* closet and watched closely while Landry picked out his clothes. "Less swanky tonight?"

"Tonight I'm going for carefully cultivated casual."

"Ah. I still think you should wear that sweater more. The one that matches your eyes."

Apparently flirtation was still going to make Landry blush, even though they'd slept together. He had always sucked at flirting. Jordan's playfulness was new to him— and Landry was discovering he liked it.

Tonight's restaurant was downtown, a couple of blocks from the Denny's but in an entirely different

culinary category. It was called Re/Style, complete
with cutesy and unnecessary punctuation.

"Ah," Jordan muttered as soon as they entered.
"Hipster food."

He wasn't wrong. The place claimed to serve
"reimagined comforting classics in refreshed ways."
After perusing the menu and looking around, Landry
concluded this meant thirty bucks for a BLT made with
rainbow bread, kale, and candied bacon. With artisanal
pickles on the side. Re/Style didn't offer alcohol but
instead focused on cold-pressed juices.

"At least we don't need a microscope to see our
dinner," Jordan said cheerfully. He ordered a trendy
permutation of grilled cheese with tomato soup, while
Landry decided on fried chicken. Their waiter, a young
man named Humberto, was adorable, with big sparkly
earrings and deep dimples.

"He recognizes you."

Landry looked at Jordan in surprise. "How do you
know? He didn't say anything."

"Yeah, he's too much of a pro for that. But watch
how he interacts with other people. He fussed over us
way more."

Landry watched and saw the truth of Jordan's
statement. While Humberto was a good waiter in general,
he didn't spend as much time at the other tables.

"Maybe he just thinks you're cute," Landry said.

"Maybe he thinks *you're* cute. But nah. I can tell."
Jordan looked thoughtful. "It's rough, isn't it? Not
being anonymous."

"I chose my career path. I'm not going to complain."

"Sure. But when you chose it, did you truly realize
what it would mean?"

Landry replied with a shrug. He hadn't given the price of fame much thought when he was younger, and to the extent he did consider it, he'd thought it was a small price. After all, look what he had. Look how many people admired him, hung on his every word. That was worth a lack of privacy, wasn't it?

Their food arrived promptly but in surprising forms. Landry's chicken legs sat on their ends in a flower pot, tied together by braided garlic chives: a poultry bouquet. A vegetable medley overflowed the scoop of a plastic spade, and the accompanying roll was shaped like a worm or caterpillar, complete with currant eyes. Humberto served the entire ensemble on a tray illustrated with antique seed packets.

Jordan received his soup in a small black cauldron. A rack arched over the cauldron, with the grilled cheese suspended from hooks and dripping into the soup.

"It's like a sandwich torture chamber," Jordan said. He picked up a slender fried zucchini stick and stabbed it into his bread. "Confess or it's the esophagus for you!"

"What crimes might your dinner have committed?"

"Burning the roof of someone's mouth? Hmm. Maybe getting grease all over their fingers, which then touched expensive clothes or important papers."

"How dastardly!"

Jordan tore off a hunk of sandwich and ate it. "You know what's really dastardly? Someone in the kitchen has to wash all these stupid-assed shovels and things. Plates were invented for a reason."

That was a good point, and Landry made a mental note to never recommend overly cutesy serving ideas. He dug into his meal, which was tasty but not spectacular. He would have been almost as satisfied with the chicken that came in a cardboard bucket.

Humberto checked in with them often, topping off their water glasses and bringing a felled forest's worth of extra napkins. He whisked away their empty dishes promptly, and when they declined dessert, he promised to bring coffee instead.

"I really hope it comes in a regular cup," Jordan said after Humberto was gone.

Before Landry could speculate on how else the restaurant could serve coffee, a woman strode purposefully toward them. Her dark hair was pinned up, and around her waist was a white apron suspiciously free of food splatters.

"Mr. Bishop?" Although her smile was wide, it looked strained.

Landry shook her outstretched hand. "Landry Bishop. And this is Jordan Stryker."

She barely glanced Jordan's way. "I'm Ivory Wintuck. Owner-chef of Re/Style. I'm so honored to have you as a guest!"

What followed was fifteen minutes of awkward conversation in which Landry tried to say kind things about her restaurant without outright lying while repeatedly turning down offers to try the rest of the menu items. He kept trying to include Jordan in the chatter, but Ivory mostly ignored him. Jordan simply watched.

Finally Landry had enough. "Thanks for visiting with us, Ivory. It's been a pleasure. But Jordan and I would like to continue our date."

Her eyes widened. "Oh! I thought— Never mind. Thank you again, Landry." After a brief negotiation in which she offered to comp their entire bill and Landry politely refused, she wished him good night, gave

Jordan a final glance, and walked away. They never did get their coffee.

"Sorry about that," muttered Landry. But Jordan was giving him an odd look, piercing and undecipherable. Landry paid the check and led them out onto the street. He intended to call for a ride back to the hotel, but Jordan leaned against a nearby brick wall and stared at him.

"What?" Landry finally demanded.

"You told her we were dating."

"You didn't want me to?"

"No, it's fine. But you could have said I was your PA. It would have been the truth."

Flummoxed, Landry shook his head. "Not the whole truth. Anyway, why does it matter what I told her? She was incredibly rude to you."

"I don't care about that. I'm just...." He looked away, as if fascinated by the blinking lights on the bar down the street. His bouncing and his pursed lips betrayed his anxiety, however, and eventually he looked at Landry again. "You don't mind if people know you and I are... a thing. Of some kind."

Landry decided they could name the thing later. He moved closer and cupped Jordan's chin. "Why on earth would I mind?"

"I'm not exactly in your league, am I? I'm not a celebrity or a rich lawyer or... anything like that. I'm kind of a flake who's never done anything important."

Oh no. Regret and self-damnation flooded Landry. "I'm so sorry if I gave you the impression I didn't think you were good enough for me. I *never* felt that way. It's not why I was reluctant. You are nobody to be ashamed of. Not ever."

"Yeah?" Hesitancy was rare for Jordan, and it broke Landry's heart a little. Had nobody ever told him he was valuable?

"Yes. And you told me yourself that what you want to do is make other people's lives easier. That's at least as important as writing blogs about brightening your living room with fresh throw pillow covers."

They kissed then, of course. A warm kiss, sweet as honey and filled with promise. Tonight Landry didn't much care about hiding public displays of affection. He wanted Jordan to know his words were sincere, and he couldn't think of better proof. Judging by the way Jordan's shoulders relaxed under Landry's hands, he found the kiss persuasive.

Soon afterward they caught a ride back to the hotel, practically sprinted to the elevator, and made out during the fast ride up. Inside the suite, they sent their clothes flying. One of Landry's shoes knocked a snack container off the display stand, no doubt activating the automated inventory. He'd end up being billed for those snacks, but what did it matter? Especially when he learned that Jordan's purchases that afternoon included condoms and lube and that Jordan was eager to use them in whichever ways Landry saw fit.

Once again, Landry took the lead. Not because he was a control freak, not because he was used to giving orders, and certainly not because Jordan showed hesitance in any way—because he most definitely did not. Landry took charge because he delighted in exploring Jordan's body and finding new ways to make him moan. Jordan was a willing feast, and Landry was ravenous.

After some preparation and Jordan's demands that he hurry up, Landry sank into Jordan's body. Groaning, Jordan stared up at him and urged him deeper. Harder.

And when it all became too much and Landry lost his rhythm, simply plunging onward without finesse, Jordan pulled Landry's head down and sighed into his ear. "Perfect, Lan. God, perfect."

By nine thirty, they lay naked, sweaty, and sated in Landry's bed. Although tempted to turn in—with Jordan—Landry sat up and sighed. "I have to—"

"Get some work done." Jordan said it without rancor but looked disappointed. "Gotcha."

"We'll want an early start in the morning."

"Do you want me to pack up everything tonight?"

"It can wait. Relax."

"I'd tell you the same, but you won't listen. Hang on, though." Still delightfully bare, Jordan padded out of the bedroom and into his own. He returned a moment later carrying what looked like folded clothes. "Here. Put these on."

"Why? What are they?"

"Don't sound so suspicious. I promise they won't make you burst into flames."

Landry took the items with a degree of trepidation. One of them turned out to be a purple T-shirt bearing the iconic Welcome to Fabulous Las Vegas sign. The other was a pair of black sweatpants made of very soft cotton fleece. Landry held one item in each hand. "Why?"

"They're comfy. You don't need to dress up when you're working in a hotel room."

Landry *always* dressed up. With rare exceptions over the past years, the closest he'd come to casual was wearing Jordan's T-shirt. But as usual he found Jordan hard to resist, so he donned the new outfit. "The shirt's too big."

"When you go out, you can wear stuff that shows off your physique. I already know what's hidden under there"—he gave a wolfish smile—"and a baggy shirt is perfect for when you want to be schlumpy and relaxed."

As Landry sat in the living room, he had to admit that the soft, roomy T-shirt felt nice. Sometimes he stroked the leg of the sweatpants, enjoying the sueded feel of the fabric. In his bedroom—*their* bedroom now—Jordan sprawled naked in bed, laughing quietly at whatever he was watching on TV. That was nice too. Much better than the instrumental music Landry sometimes piped through his speakers in an attempt to feel less alone.

Tomorrow they'd return to a more normal routine in LA, and Landry wasn't at all certain what shape their relationship would take then. For now, though, he was content with what he had.

That warm feeling accompanied him through several texts and a few emails. Until he got to a message that began *Dear Wormy, You need to come back to Peril.*

Chapter Twelve

"WHY won't they tell you what's up?" Jordan asked.

They'd passed over the California state line many miles back, and now he piloted the Benz past scattered Joshua trees. Westbound traffic was annoyingly heavy, yet he maintained open car lengths between the Benz and the car in front of them. When other drivers inevitably cut in, he never once called them names. He seemed much more interested in Landry's news from Nebraska than in getting home.

"I don't know," Landry whined. "To torture me."

"Or tempt you."

Landry snorted. As if anything in Nebraska could tempt him.

A BMW zoomed into their lane so abruptly that Jordan had to brake, but he didn't even flip the guy off. "Do you have any inkling what's going on in Peril?"

"Missy says our aunt Trudy is scheming something that involves me, but that doesn't narrow it down. She could be up to anything. Once, when I was twelve, she bought a bunch of cans of paint at the hardware store in Alliance. They were on clearance, and every can was a different color. She made all the cousins come over to her place, and then she split us into teams and gave each team a room and a can of paint. She timed us to see who could finish their room first."

"Did your team win?"

"Yes," Landry said, chuckling. "We got Dairy Queen as our reward."

"Well, that doesn't sound painful."

"Another time she ended up with about a million yards of the most godawful dinosaur-print flannel fabric. She made us all pajamas with it. And took our pictures wearing them. *That* was painful."

"A fate worse than death."

Okay, it hadn't actually been too awful. She'd also hosted a slumber party for everyone that night, with popcorn and cupcakes and scary movies on her TV. Landry's cousin Bob, two years older and with a tendency to bully, had screamed louder than anyone when the alien burst out of the crewman's chest. That scream had been entirely satisfying.

"Aunt Trudy sounds like a lot of fun," said Jordan, slowing as he neared a lumbering RV.

"She's a force of nature." Then Landry remembered something he never should have forgotten. "She's the one who encouraged me to apply to colleges outside Nebraska. She helped me with the applications and everything. Almost everyone else was trying to convince me that Omaha would be plenty exotic enough."

"And what does she expect from you now?"

"Dunno. Missy tells me Aunt Trudy keeps saying I'm a good role model, whatever that means."

"So you have to go, then."

Ugh. "I guess. After I finish taping the *Suzee Show*." Hesitantly, he added, "Do you want to come with?"

"As your boyfriend or PA?"

Boyfriend. Huh. Had they progressed that far? Landry supposed so, and the knowledge was surprisingly satisfying. "Both."

Ah. A ten on the Stryker Scale. "Cool!"

"It is not cool. It's the polar opposite of cool—no pun intended. If there were a contest for the least interesting, most prosaic place on the planet, Peril would be an excellent contender. The banality of the town knows no bounds. So don't expect to be charmed or amused by Peril."

"I get to meet your family, right?"

Landry sighed. "Yes."

"Then I'm not so sure about the no-amusement clause."

Landry didn't bother to argue. Soon enough, Jordan would see for himself.

TODD listened earnestly as Landry explained the next segment. Again.

"Your part in this is completely uncomplicated."

"Sure, boss. I just carry in that little table. Easy-peasy." Todd flexed an arm muscle, maybe to demonstrate his ability to haul furniture, or maybe just out of habit. He undoubtedly flexed in his sleep.

"You carry in the little table, you set it in front of the guest, and you smile at the audience."

"They do like it when I smile."

"They do indeed. And after you smile, you open the cabinet beneath the table, take out the gift-wrapped box, and set it on the tabletop. You are welcome to add flourishes and flexes, if you care to. Then you exit, stage left."

"Got it."

"*Don't* trip over the power cables this time."

"I won't." Landry had reached the final day of his five-day run as guest host, and so far things had run pretty smoothly. In the segment on using masa harina, the show's kitchen staff had burned the pupusas and there wasn't time to make another batch. So Landry improvised a poblano sauce, which he poured over the scorched bits, and he took big bites while pretending he wasn't eating charcoal. Nobody in the studio audience seemed to notice, which was good. Another day, Todd had done a face-plant just as he went offstage. But he wasn't injured, and again Landry extemporized, this time doing an impromptu lesson on first aid. The show went on.

Now all he had to do was get through a segment on making cookie cups from which to drink sweet Kahlua shots, look amused as a stand-up comedian did a brief bit, and then interview Dain Kilpatrick, an up-and-coming actor pimping his new rom-com. Easy.

As Landry watched the studio audience chat among themselves before the show, Jordan emerged from backstage with a bottle of water. Some of the audience members cheered and clapped. Over the past week, people had cottoned on to the fact that Jordan was more than just a PA, and that seemed to have sparked enthusiasm. Yesterday one of the show's interns had informed Landry of the existence of Landry/Jordan fanfic, a fact Landry tried hard to unknow.

"Want anything else?" asked Jordan, handing Landry the bottle. "Something to eat?"

"No, thank you. We can go out after we finish here."

"Fancy-schmancy or casual?"

"I was thinking pizza, actually." A few slices of cheese-and-pepperoni-laden indulgence might help alleviate some stress even as it reminded him he was an ordinary mortal.

"Perfect. I got our flight booked to Nebraska and a rental car once we arrive. Man, it's not easy getting to Peril."

"Or escaping," Landry said darkly.

Jordan ignored him. "We change planes in Denver, then we get a puddle jumper to Scottsbluff. Does that sound okay?"

"It's fine."

"What about lodging?"

Landry waved his arms theatrically. "Book us the penthouse suite at the Peril Ritz."

"Hmm. I was gonna get us a room at the Byway Inn, which I learned is the only choice in town. But then Missy emailed—"

"Oh no."

"—and we're staying with her."

Landry deeply regretted having given those two each other's email addresses. They'd been sending messages back and forth for days. "She has four-year-old twins."

"Who have never met their Uncle Landry. Anyway, she says her house is plenty big enough, and also the Byway Inn is a dump."

Both statements were true. The Byway had been a dump when Landry left Peril, and he doubted the intervening years had been kind. Missy lived in the house they'd grown up in, an early twentieth-century structure that had suffered multiple additions built by generations of Bishops. It would be far more family togetherness than he'd experienced in a long time.

"We could probably—"

"Landry. You know perfectly well there are no good alternatives, plus you're going to hurt Missy's feelings if you stay anywhere else. You're on thin ice with her as it is."

It occurred to Landry that if Jordan had been simply his PA, he wouldn't have voiced these thoughts so strongly. But Jordan was more than that, of course. And maybe those thoughts needed to be voiced.

"Okay," he said quietly.

"Um… I haven't exactly told her that you and I are a thing."

"Why not?"

"I figured she's your sister—you should decide what and when to disclose."

Landry took a big swig of water and then blotted his mouth with the back of his hand. "She knows I'm gay. When I was seven I used to steal her Barbies and make them stunning little ensembles out of fabric scraps. Now, I admit, that didn't guarantee I'd grow up liking boys, but the odds were in my favor."

"She knows you're into guys in general, but she doesn't know you're into me specifically. Um, unless she reads the fanfic."

Landry shuddered. "As far as I know, Missy pays little or no attention to my professional life. I doubt anyone in Peril cares about my career, in fact." After another hefty swallow, he handed the bottle back to Jordan. "Anyway, you can tell her if you want to. If you don't, we're going to end up in separate bedrooms."

"The horror!"

Jordan was joking, but Landry was at least somewhat serious. He and Jordan hadn't slept apart since they returned from Vegas, and he'd already become accustomed to Jordan's big, warm body in his bed. Even when they weren't touching, he liked to listen to Jordan breathing, a reminder that he wasn't alone in the world.

The stage manager approached, clipboard in hand, her ponytail as closely regimented as always. She ran a tight ship, which Landry admired. She pointed the clipboard at him. "Ready?"

"I think so."

Jordan leaned in to give Landry a peck on the cheek. "Break a leg. And not by tripping over something."

Within minutes Landry was seated onstage in one of the red armchairs. Suzee had ordered them custom-made for the show, wanting to make sure that she and her guests could sit comfortably with no temptation to slump. Jordan had chosen outfits that looked good against the fabric and fit the informal vibe Suzee's viewers were used to. Today Landry wore the turquoise sweater and a pair of charcoal trousers.

After a round of spirited clapping from the audience, Landry smiled out at them. "Many of you first saw my next guest when he burned up your Instagram feed. Now he's proving that he acts even better than he poses. He's currently starring as a lovelorn veterinarian in *Bark If You Love Me*. Please welcome Dain Kilpatrick!"

Dain sauntered onto the set, waving at the audience as he walked. When he reached Landry, who'd stood to greet him, they shook hands and then sat.

"Thanks so much for coming here today," Landry said.

"It's a pleasure."

Landry hadn't known him previously, but they'd had a few minutes to chat before the show. Dain seemed nice enough, if a little vain. He'd asked Landry for tips on skin-care products—seeming to truly want the advice, not just flattering Landry—and he'd recommended a restaurant in his hometown of Charleston. He'd also flirted a little, but Landry hadn't responded in kind. He had no interest in a closeted actor, especially now that he had Jordan.

But now, with people watching and the cameras focused their way, the conversation was light and easy. Dain told an amusing story about getting locked out of a hotel room wearing nothing but a towel, then an anecdote about a modeling gig he endured while recovering from food poisoning. The audience ate him up.

"Let's talk a little bit about your movie, Dain."

"What? I have a new movie coming out right when I'm booked on your show? What a coincidence!"

"It's uncanny. In *Bark If You Love Me*, you play a man who's better with animals than with humans."

"Right, right. I'm sort of a pet whisperer, but when it comes to people—especially women—I can barely function. But then this pretty young woman inherits her cat-lady grandmother's houseful of felines and, well, love might find a way."

At one time, Landry's smile in response to such talk of love would have been entirely manufactured. But lately some of his cynicism had rubbed away. Sometimes maybe love *did* find a way. Temporarily, anyway, and that was far better than not at all.

"It sounds very sweet," Landry said.

"It was a joy to film. The cast, the crew—everyone was fantastic. Even the critters. I know W.C. Fields said never to work with animals or children, but I had a great time."

"And I think we have a clip. Would you like to set it up?"

The audience roared at the scene, a cute one in which the love interest watches while the vet gives an enema to a boa constrictor. The movie wasn't really to Landry's taste, but he wondered if maybe Jordan would enjoy it. Landry hadn't been out to a fluffy popcorn-and-Junior-Mints flick in years.

When the clip ended and the house lights came up, Dain looked pleased. "I'd never handled a snake before we shot that. It was pretty cool, except he kept trying to slither down the back of my shirt. It tickled."

Landry waited for the laughter to ebb. "So you don't mind creepy-crawlies?"

"Not snakes, no. And anything with four legs is cool. But once you start adding more legs than that, well, things get a little dicey for me."

"Understandable. Dain, we have a surprise for you."

"I love surprises." Dain rubbed his hands together. "Good. Todd?"

Right on cue, Todd entered the set carrying the small table. As always, the crowd cheered and whistled. He managed not to trip over anything, and in fact he made it all the way to Dain without mishap, then set the table carefully in place. He made a little show of bending to retrieve the gift box, deliberately aiming his well-formed posterior toward the appreciative audience and even giving it the tiniest of waggles. He placed the box atop the table, waved to the crowd, tipped a wink to Landry, and exited. Without a single disaster.

Landry hoped the cameras didn't pick up his probable look of relief.

"What's this?" Dain asked, looking at the brightly wrapped box. He knew perfectly well what was inside—a realistic rubber tarantula—because Landry had told him before the show. The producer had wanted to make it a true surprise, but Landry didn't believe in terrorizing guests. He also preferred to control the set as much as possible. If a guest was truly shocked, any kind of chaos might break out.

"It's just a little gift," Landry said.

Moving a bit overtheatrically, Dain untied the large bow and lifted the lid. As planned, the sides of the box collapsed outwards, revealing an enormous furry spider. Dain shouted quite credibly and lurched backward. The audience roared.

And then the spider *moved.*

A lot of things happened at once. Dain shrieked and scrambled backward over the chair, causing it to overturn. He fell to the ground with the chair on top of him. The audience members screamed. Landry leapt to his feet just in time to watch the tarantula skitter off the table and toward the front of the stage. Unsure what to do first, he made the split-second decision to extricate Dain. And Todd—oh, bless him—sprinted onto the set, scooped the spider into his huge hands just before it fell over the edge, and raced away into the wings.

Chapter Thirteen

"I AM *so* sorry," the producer said for the umpteenth time. It was unclear whether he was talking to Dain, who was holding an ice pack to his face, or to Landry, who was imagining creative ways to cause the producer pain. Landry was, in fact, in imminent danger of testing one of those methods when Jordan stepped in.

"I think you better give Mr. Bishop some space," Jordan said to the producer. "And maybe have a chat with your lawyer."

"I thought it would be *funny*. More genuine!"

Jordan made a shooing motion and, after watching the producer trudge away, turned to Landry. "Are you all right?"

"Ask Dain. He's the one who landed on his face."

Dain waved a dismissive hand. "I'm okay." His voice sounded nasal. "But do you think they'll air that bit?"

Landry sighed. He didn't want to tape another segment, but without that final interview, the show would be too short. "We'll replace it with something, don't worry."

"No, don't! If you show it, I bet it goes viral. Great publicity for the movie."

"Are you sure you're okay with that?"

"Sure, whatever. Any publicity is good publicity, right? Besides, my character's supposed to be kind of bumbling, so…." He spread his arms. His nose and one eye were turning interesting shades of red and purple.

"Thank you for being so good-natured about this. I assure you, I didn't—"

"Didn't know the fucker was gonna be real. I believe ya."

Jordan gave a satisfied nod and spoke to Landry. "You're not freaking out?"

"No." Landry dropped his voice to a whisper. "But we're going to need to stop for hamburgers on the way home. Greasy ones with bacon. And milkshakes."

"Done. And after we get home, you'll put on your Vegas sweats and we'll binge-watch *The Simpsons*." He gave Landry's shoulder a squeeze. "In the meantime, excuse me while I go rip that producer and his minions a new one."

"Not Todd. I don't think he knew about the spider either. And he stopped it from getting into the audience."

Jordan grinned. "Not only that, but he actually saved the little guy's life. It's now safe and sound, back in its cage, and it's got a hell of a story to tell its grandspiders someday." He squeezed Landry's shoulder again and kissed him for good measure, then walked purposefully in the direction the producer had gone.

"I wish I had a PA like that," Dain said wistfully.

"He's my boyfriend."

"Even better." Dain prodded cautiously at his nose and winced. "The whole work-personal intersection isn't a drag?"

"We're new."

"Well, good luck with it. Seems like he's a keeper, huh?"

"It's looking that way."

SUZEE phoned that evening, just after Landry and Jordan finished the last of the curly fries and as they were getting ready to cuddle on the couch.

"Voicemail," Jordan pleaded.

"This will be quick, I promise." He answered and turned the phone on speaker mode.

Suzee called her producer a lot of swear words and apologized for what had happened. Landry told her not to worry about it. She hadn't known anything about the tarantula swap before it happened, and anyway, most of his anger had drained away. Now he was full and sleepy, and all he really wanted was time alone with Jordan.

"Look," she said. "This isn't the best time for this, but I've been meaning to talk to you."

Uh-oh. "It can wait until you return."

"No, I want you thinking about this. Now, don't tell a soul, okay? Nobody knows. But I'm considering retiring."

"Oh." That wasn't what he'd expected her to say. "But you're so young!"

"Thank you, darling. But I'm nowhere near as young as I used to be. And the show... well, I love it. I love doing it. But it's exhausting. As I'm sure you've noticed. I'd like to spend more time with my family and explore some other interests. And I'd like to get the hell out of LA. I'm considering a charming villa in Napa. It has vineyards."

Landry ignored Jordan's gesture to finish the call. "That sounds great, but we'll miss you."

"What I want you to consider, darling, is taking over permanently. It's time for a younger, fresher voice anyway, and I know the *Landry Show* would be a big hit."

"I don't—"

"Just think about it. Tonight's not good anyway. Too post-traumatic. Mull it over and we'll talk terms when I get back."

Feeling slightly numb, Landry heard himself agree and thank her. Then they exchanged goodbyes and he set the phone aside.

Jordan gazed at him, eyes big but mouth turned down slightly at the corners. "That's an amazing opportunity, isn't it?" he asked.

"Yes."

"National audience. Tons of money. Endorsement deals out the wing-wang. Fancy parties with A-list movers and shakers. Yachts? Private jets?"

"I... I believe you're overstating matters."

"But still."

"But still." Landry sighed. "I dreamed of this when I was a kid. Being famous, I mean. I even knew what my celebrity nickname would be: Mr. Martha."

Jordan set a hand on Landry's thigh. "As in Martha Stewart?"

"I was going to have two lines of housewares. Bishop would be for upscale department stores like Neiman Marcus." Of course at that point in his life, he hadn't been within eight hundred miles of a Neiman Marcus. "And the other line would be called Landry, and they'd sell it at Walmart and Svoboda Ranch and Home, so that every couch in Peril would sport a Landry throw blanket and every kitchen would have a Landry toaster."

"You could do that, right? If you took over Suzee's show?"

"Yes. Maybe. I don't know. I…. Let's watch TV, okay?"

Jordan snuggled close and handed him the remote. But before Landry could click anything, Jordan snatched it back. "Do you want advice?"

"I don't know." Landry tipped his head back and shut his eyes. "I don't think I know anything anymore. If I ever did. Steve used to… he'd guide me."

"It's great that you had someone to do that for you. Maybe if I'd had a guide, I wouldn't have floated so aimlessly through my twenties."

Landry spent a few minutes considering what would have happened if he hadn't met Steve. No mansion with a Jag in the garage. No talk shows. No trips to New York to meet with people in the fashion world and go on TV. No book deals? He wasn't sure about that part. He'd still have his blog, though. He'd be helping people with their wardrobe and with entertaining. Maybe he'd be perfectly happy. Although he wouldn't have a PA, and that meant no Jordan.

"I think floating is perfectly acceptable in one's twenties. It's a period when many people are attempting to find their identity and place in the world." He sighed, aware he was channeling Lord Thistlebottom again. "Better than still being uncertain of those things in one's midthirties."

"Well, I think self-image is always open to alteration, at every age." Jordan was already scrunched up close, but now he wrapped an arm around Landry's shoulders and squeezed. "And that was gonna be my advice, actually. Forget about what you think you should be or what anyone else thinks you should be. Your heart knows what path it wants—you just gotta find that path and follow it."

Landry opened his eyes and turned his head toward Jordan. They were nose to nose. "That's good advice."

"I didn't invent it. Somebody gave it to me, in fact."

"Yeah? Who?"

Jordan traced Landry's lips with his thumb. "Elaine. Right before I applied to work for you."

Before Landry had fully processed that information, Jordan slid off the couch, separated Landry's knees, and scooted between them. Grinning wickedly, he untied the drawstring of Landry's sweatpants. Quick as a wink, Landry sat bare-assed on the couch, his sweats and underwear tossed aside.

"We can move—" he began.

Jordan stilled him with a warm palm cupping Landry's balls. "Nope. We're gonna do this right here."

"But—"

"Lie back, Lan. Relax. Give me permission to make all your decisions for the rest of the evening. I'm declaring you one hundred percent responsibility-free."

All his decisions. Wouldn't it be lovely to just hand everything over like that? To scoot over and let someone else drive, and not even tell him where to go or how to get there? But life wasn't like that. An adult had to maintain control of himself. Except... maybe Landry could ease up a little? Just for now.

"You don't have to... cater to me," Landry said.

Jordan removed his hand from Landry's crotch and clutched both of Landry's shoulders. He wasn't smiling, and his eyes glittered with intensity. "This isn't catering to you. Can't you tell? This is what I want too. I'm being totally selfish. 'Cause tonight I want to feel you. Taste you. And I want to watch while you finally let go—and know that *I* did that."

Nothing in the world could make Landry say no to this.

He gave just a tiny nod, but that was enough to bring back Jordan's grin, to make Jordan hold him more tightly and crush their mouths together in a ravenous kiss. And a moment later, it was enough to cause Jordan to begin licking at Landry's urgently hard cock.

Despite his acquiescence, Landry couldn't do *nothing*. So he reached out and laced his fingers through Jordan's soft hair. Jordan hummed his approval.

There was something deliciously dirty about this scenario: Landry half-naked and sprawled wantonly on his expensive couch, Jordan fully dressed and bowed over Landry's groin, clever tongue and agile fingers busy at their task. Lord Thistlebottom would never enjoy this. Oh, but Landry *was* enjoying. Every bit of hot, wet suction. Every inch of probing pressure. He scooted his ass down a little, spread his legs as wide as possible, tipped his head back against the cushions, and let go.

He howled when he came.

Afterward, dazed and melty, he allowed Jordan to lead him to the bedroom. Landry stood while Jordan finished undressing him, and he watched as Jordan stripped too. Then Jordan tumbled him into bed. He plowed into Landry's tingling, compliant body until both of them were too sated to move.

Landry didn't get up to brush his teeth and do his bedtime skin-care ritual. He didn't even bother to deal with the sticky mess on their bodies. He simply allowed Jordan to hold him close, Landry's head pillowed on his chest. He fell asleep listening to Jordan's strong heartbeat.

Chapter Fourteen

"I'M never going to be content to fly the cheap seats again."

Squirming in the plastic airport chair between flights, Landry peered at Jordan over his phone. "Well, set your sights lower, because there's no first class on the next plane."

"No warm chocolate chip cookies?" Jordan grinned.

"We'll be lucky if it has engines instead of frantically flapping pigeons."

Jordan's snorts of laughter lifted a bit of the anxiety from Landry's shoulders, but just a bit. Honestly, if he thought he could get away with it, he'd board the next flight back to LA. But he knew that if necessary, Jordan would drag him down the Jetway and onto their tiny little Scottsbluff-bound plane. Why had he agreed to this trip

to begin with? Surely he could have found some excuse
to stay in LA. A home-furnishings emergency, perhaps.
An important meeting with a pop diva who needed tips
on theming her shih tzu's engagement party. A pressing
need to invent new Thanksgiving mocktails.

Ugh.

"It's almost time," Jordan pointed out. "Want
anything before we leave civilization?"

"Ah, you mock. But have you ever been to western
Nebraska?"

"Never been to Nebraska at all. But I *have* been to
Lind, Washington. Several times. Had family there and
we'd go visit sometimes. The social event of the year in
Lind is a demolition derby with farm combines, and the
second big entertainment is watching wheat grow."

Landry grunted. It sounded as if Lind might have
certain similarities to Peril. "So then you know."

"Eh. People are still people, whether in LA or Lind.
And even Lind has all the basics of life. Electricity,
running water, Diet Coke… the whole shebang."

Unconvinced, and fighting the temptation to indulge
in the savory soft pretzels he'd spied nearby, Landry
returned his attention to his phone. Suzee's producer had
sent him yet another apology. Landry texted back that he
should stop saying he was sorry and give Todd a raise
instead. His literary agent was checking on the book's
progress; Landry sent a quick summary. A shoe designer
who was a friend of an acquaintance was hoping to meet
Landry sometime soon. She was certain he was going to
love what she'd been doing with espadrilles. A booking
agent in New York wanted to know if he was free for
another late-night talk-show visit.

Really, Landry's PA should have been handling these, but worrying about footwear meant Landry could partially ignore the gnawing in his gut.

But then it was time to board.

The flight was turbulent, which didn't seem to bother Jordan, but Landry gripped the armrests, closed his eyes, and pretended to nap. Even if he had managed to fall asleep, it wouldn't have lasted long. In almost no time at all, they were bouncing to a landing in Scottsbluff.

One good thing about a small plane was the quick disembarking process. Luggage arrived almost immediately, and Jordan took both suitcases and followed Landry across the airport's single gate to the car rental counter. Landry didn't pay attention while Jordan chatted with the rental clerk, so when they got outside and Landry saw their vehicle, he came to a halt.

"You rented a pickup truck?"

Jordan patted the driver's door. "It's a big one. Seats five, so plenty of room for our stuff."

"There would be plenty of room for our luggage in a sedan."

"Where's the fun in that? When in Rome, right?" He slapped the door again. "C'mon, let's go. Missy's waiting."

Scowling, Landry helped pile the luggage into the rear of the cab, then got into the passenger seat. He was fairly certain he hadn't ridden in a truck since he left Nebraska. SUVs, yes; pickups, no.

Fortunately the weather was warm for October. Some of the trees near the North Platte River showed fall foliage, but those bits of color disappeared as they headed east and the sun set behind them.

"I wish I could see more of the scenery," Jordan said as he drove.

"Nothing to see." That wasn't exactly true. The Sandhills had a beauty of their own, the land furred with soft grasses and curved as sensuously as a Georgia O'Keeffe painting. They were nothing like the stunning ocean vistas of Big Sur or the breathtaking majesty of towering redwoods. But there was beauty nonetheless.

During the ninety-minute drive to Peril, they passed only a handful of cars going the other way.

Landry gave Jordan directions once they reached town—not that anything in Peril was hard to find. It felt odd to be rolling down streets still familiar after all these years, almost as if the plane had transported them back in time. They passed the Byway Inn, as decrepit as ever, and Svoboda Ranch and Home. Tillerson's Ford dealership was still there. The Dairy Queen. The high school where Landry had once counted the days until he could escape. The library. The little smattering of shops that surrounded the town square, which still had the gazebo in the middle. A brightly illuminated flagpole, but with the flag taken down, probably at sunset. At the base of the pole, metal plaques with the names of Peril men who had died in the World Wars, Korea, Vietnam, Afghanistan, and Iraq.

When Landry was a kid, another plaque commemorated a supposed victory over local Lakotas in the late nineteenth century. But then a group of high school students—including Missy—had presented a formal protest to the city council stating that the Lakotas had been massacred by invading whites. The students wanted a sign to commemorate *that*. In the end, the council had achieved a sort of compromise: while they refused to erect a new sign, they did take down the old one. As best as Landry could tell in the partial darkness, the compromise still held.

At Landry's direction, Jordan turned south on Third Avenue, then east on H Street. Most of the houses were modest single-story structures with white siding and deep front porches, with a few larger four-square houses mixed in. They'd all been built a century earlier. But Missy's house was a little older and considerably larger. The darkness made it hard to discern colors, but Landry thought the house was the same pale yellow as always, with the same fish-scale trim under the roofline and the same agglomeration of additions ruining whatever symmetry the original house had once possessed.

After Jordan parked on the street, Landry simply sat there. He would have willingly stayed put for a long time, maybe until he finally ordered Jordan to take them back to Scottsbluff. But the front door burst open and a flood of people rushed toward them, and it was too late to run away.

"Home," Landry mumbled.

EVERYBODY talked at once. Missy and Rod, her bear of a husband. Aunt Trudy. Ten thousand first cousins plus assorted seconds and once-removeds. And of course Missy's twins, Blake and Bryanna, who'd taken an immediate shine to Jordan. He sat in the living room in the middle of it all, seemingly as pleased as punch, with children hanging off him and a smile on his face.

Landry, however, was cowering. Okay, maybe not quite. He sat on a ratty old armchair, his late father's favorite spot for watching TV football. Yet even though the chair was in a corner, people loomed over him, asking a few questions but mostly bombarding him with every notable event in Peril since his exit. Who'd been married, had kids, divorced. Who'd gotten hired or fired. Old businesses that had closed and new ones that had opened. A panoply of illnesses, accidents, and natural disasters.

As if the flood of talking wasn't enough to overwhelm him, Landry was constantly surprised by how *old* everyone had become. His cousin Terry, for instance, was ten years Landry's senior and, when Landry was in high school, had a reputation for living wild. Back then he lived in a trailer on his parents' property and spent most of his time wandering the highways on his motorcycle. He would rumble back into Peril with a girl perched behind him, she and Terry would spend a couple of weeks drinking and dancing at a bar, and then she'd leave—only to be replaced a few weeks later. Now Terry was married to someone he'd gone to high school with, and he had a paunch, a bald spot, and a job at the Ford dealership.

Other cousins who had been toddlers when Landry left were now fully grown—he couldn't even recognize many of them—and a few already had kids of their own. Although Aunt Trudy retained every ounce of her vitality and forcefulness, she now walked with a cane and complained about her knees.

What did they see when they looked at him? Certainly not the teen who'd fled as soon as he could.

Missy saved him at last. Standing in the center of the living room, she raised her voice above the din. "Okay, okay. Enough family love for now. You'll all get plenty of Landry time, I promise. Now everyone go home so we can feed him."

Although it took some time for people to gather coats and say their goodbyes, they ultimately obeyed, and blessed silence settled over the house. Except for the Disney movie the twins watched at full blast—but

Landry much preferred "Let It Go" to the chorus of cousins. Jordan and Rod sat together on the couch, deep in conversation; Landry wondered what the topic was. He had met Rod only once, when he and Missy made a honeymoon trip to Disneyland, but Landry liked the guy. He was originally from Rapid City, South Dakota, but had come to Peril to teach high school. Apparently he'd liked the place—and Missy—enough to stay.

Missy poked Landry's shoulder. "Come help me with dinner."

They walked into the kitchen together, and Landry took a good look around. "Nice job. I like it."

"Really?" Missy seemed a little shy at his praise.

"Really. Did you design it yourself?"

"Rod and I did together. We did most of the work too. We pulled out all the fugly seventies stuff Grandma and Grandpa put in, but the cabinets are the originals."

Landry stroked the painted wood on a cupboard door. "I love how well you integrated the modern touches without losing the vintage appeal. Well done."

"Wow. *The* Landry Bishop likes my kitchen." She fanned herself with one hand and pretended to swoon.

"You look good too. I didn't get a chance to say that before the hordes descended."

She looked doubtfully down at her torso. "I've put on weight."

"It suits you." He meant it. She wore jeans and a Deadpool sweatshirt, and her hair had undoubtedly been cut by their great-aunt Pat, who'd been cutting hair at her salon downtown since mammoths roamed the plains. But Missy looked happy and confident and comfortable with herself, and that made her beautiful.

"Well, thanks. I bet you don't weigh an ounce more than you did when you left here."

"It's LA. They monitor those things."

She snorted, opened the fridge, and began pulling items out. "Thing One and Thing Two ate already. Which is fine, because the only foods they'll willingly consume right now are cheese pizza, Tater Tots, and those packaged fruit snacks. And apples, but only if they're peeled and sliced."

"That sounds healthy."

"Eh. I give 'em vitamins." She grabbed a salad bowl and pushed it at him. "Besides, next week they'll demand a totally different menu. It all balances in the end."

He wasn't so sure about that, but parenting was not one of his areas of expertise. So instead of saying anything, he gathered the vegetables she pointed out to him, took them to the kitchen island, and began to prepare a salad.

In the meantime, Missy placed a baking dish into the oven. "I mixed it ahead of time, so it'll be ready in half an hour."

"Is that Mom's tuna and green bean casserole?" Landry's stomach growled.

"Yep. I even have the goldfish crackers to sprinkle on top. I hope you weren't expecting something Californian and fancy."

"No, the casserole is great. I haven't had it since… since Mom died. But if you want, I can make dinner tomorrow. Something exotic." He wasn't sure what ingredients he'd be able to find at the Barn Owl Market, but he'd surely manage something.

"That'd be nice. Aunt Trudy's thing is at one o'clock tomorrow, by the way. You brought a suit, right?"

"Yes. You told Jordan I'd need one. But what *is* Aunt Trudy's thing?"

"Nope. Sworn to secrecy."

"C'mon, Miss." He barely kept a whine out of his tone.

"Let's just say that maybe you're not the only one who grew up feeling different in Peril. And let's also just say that maybe Aunt Trudy and some other people decided those distinctive kids might need a little extra... something."

Her hints did little to relieve his bewilderment. "What does that mean?"

"You'll find out tomorrow, Wormy." She stood next to him, grabbed the carrots he'd peeled, and began to chop them. But even out of the corner of his eye, Landry could tell she was watching him.

"What?" he demanded after a few moments.

"It must be awfully nice having a personal assistant. I'd love to have someone run things to the post office and take the twins to the dentist."

"He does a lot more than that."

"Hmm."

Landry scowled because that was the precise noise their mother had made when she suspected one of her children was feeding her bullshit. "He does! He sets my appointments, taxis me wherever I need to go, deals with things like the yard service and the housecleaners. He takes care of all the details so I can concentrate on my work."

"You work really hard, don't you?"

He stopped peeling and looked at her in surprise. He'd assumed people in Peril had the impression that his life was a whirlwind of fabulous parties and hobnobbing with the stars. "I do."

"Maybe too hard."

That made him narrow his eyes. "Have you been talking to Jordan about this?"

"Nope." She popped a piece of carrot in her mouth. "I just know you."

"Oh."

"But this is interesting. Does Jordan think you work too hard?"

Landry shrugged, moved the last of the carrots toward her, and reached for the lettuce. "Iceberg."

"Unless you're the Titanic, it won't kill you, Wormy."

He began to tear it into appropriately sized pieces. "Other kinds of lettuce taste better. And other greens have better nutritional value."

"I like the way iceberg crunches. Don't look at me like that. We get the farm-to-table boxes during the summer, but this time of year we get what's on sale at Barn Owl."

He nodded, hopeful that he'd successfully changed the subject. But he should have known better. One of Missy's childhood nicknames had been Pit Bull.

"So Jordan lectures you on your work habits." She'd given up all pretense of salad prep and now stood with her arms crossed. "Is that something personal assistants are supposed to do?"

"This one does." He dumped a handful of lettuce into the bowl and looked at her. "Because he's also my boyfriend."

She didn't look surprised, and the news certainly didn't upset her. In fact, she grinned and gave his bicep a light punch. "I knew it! He's great, Lan. Really sweet and funny, and I can tell that he cares a lot about you."

He discovered that her approval mattered to him. "Thanks. We're new, so I don't know where we're going, but…."

"But you're a stick-to-things kind of guy. We all are. I bet the Bishops have the lowest divorce rate of any family in Sheridan County. When we start things, we mean it. That could be our motto."

He smiled at her but wasn't convinced he should be lumped in with the rest of the Bishops. Maybe he took after their mother's family, the Keiths. There were a lot fewer of them, and with the exception of their mother, they tended toward the squirrelly. Their maternal grandfather, for example, had been positive that friendly aliens were due to arrive anytime, and he used to mow a landing pad into his wheat field in hopes they'd be attracted to his ranch first. He also ended up marrying and divorcing four times, although Landry suspected the obsession with extraterrestrials was at least partially to blame.

"Does it work out okay?" Missy asked. "Him being your assistant and your main squeeze?"

"So far. Like I said, we're new."

"Hmm."

They finished the salad, and then he helped set the table. Missy insisted they use the good china. It wasn't expensive, but it had been the set their parents reserved for special occasions. They used the kitchen table because the dining room table was occupied by an enormous half-completed jigsaw puzzle. "Rod's been working on that damn thing for centuries. The twins will be grandparents before we get to use the table again." She said it with an exasperated fondness that made him grin.

"I don't mind eating in the kitchen. I usually do at home."

"Really? I pictured you doing all your meals with tuxedos and candelabras and a grand piano."

"Oh, I much prefer a string quartet."

She bopped him in the shoulder. She used to poke and hit him a lot when they were kids, and she got away with it because she was younger, which annoyed him back then. Now, though, he recognized the mild thumps as signs of affection and kind of liked them.

"Do you want to take your stuff upstairs?" Missy asked. "Or is that Jordan's job?"

Jordan was still deep in animated discussion with Rod, each of them with a kid on his lap. Landry shook his head fondly. "I think I can manage it."

With one bag in each hand, he followed Missy upstairs, where she gave an impromptu tour. "Rod and I have Mom and Dad's old bedroom, of course."

He peeked inside. "Wow, you did a lot of work in there too."

"Well, it was pretty much an eighties time warp, so yeah."

Next she showed him her old room. It still contained the furniture from their childhood, but now the walls were a nice seafoam color and someone had added a built-in seat under the window. A zooful of stuffed animals clustered in one corner. "It's supposed to be Bryanna's," Missy explained, "but she'd rather sleep on Blake's bottom bunk. We were gonna put Jordan in here."

"Now you're not?"

"Don't you guys want to share?"

He blinked at her. "Well... yes. You're okay with that?"

"What part do you think I'm *not* okay with?" She sounded a little angry. "I'm not a bigot or a prude, Landry, and neither is Rod."

"I know. It's just weird. I never expected to share a bed under this roof with my boyfriend."

"Well, I'm glad you are, if it makes you happy."

"Thanks, Miss."

They peeked in at Blake's room, where toys, books, and clothes lay scattered on every imaginable surface. Quite a difference from when Grandma Bishop slept there. She had been inclined toward threadbare quilts and kitschy figurines. They continued to the end of the hall and Landry's old bedroom. He gasped when Missy opened the door. "It's the same!"

"Not exactly. We refinished the old hardwood floor, and the bed linens are new."

He turned around slowly, still clutching suitcases. "But the paint, the furniture…." He'd chosen the colors himself and bought the bed and dresser with money from the various part-time jobs he had during high school.

"All Landry Bishop originals. It's a beautiful room. Besides, we wanted you to feel at home if you ever came back." She gazed solemnly at him. "This will always be your home, no matter what. You know that, right?"

And he found himself beginning to believe just that.

Chapter Fifteen

THE twins complained about bedtime until Jordan offered to read them a story, and then they bounced up the stairs like rabbits. Rod went with them too, in hopes of preserving part of their routine, but he returned to the living room before Jordan did. "They've talked him into *Fox in Socks*. Poor guy."

"He's having fun with your kids, actually."

"He's great with them."

"He likes to take care of people and make them happy."

"Good catch, dude." Rod plopped down on the couch next to Missy.

Jordan eventually rejoined them, and the four of them stayed up late, just talking. Missy and Landry told tales about their childhood—most of them things Landry hadn't thought about in years. Rod responded with war stories from teaching high school biology. And Jordan talked about funny things that had happened at the many jobs he'd held. They all laughed a great deal.

Missy broke up the party with a huge yawn. "You all may be on Hollywood time, but I'm not. Bed for me. Besides, tomorrow's a big day." Her face gave nothing away.

Landry discovered he was exhausted too. Part of it was the travel and the onslaught of relatives, but partly he was emotionally drained. He hadn't expected his homecoming to elicit such a variety of feelings. Before he went upstairs, he put on his jacket and went out onto the back porch, where Jordan joined him a moment later.

"Want alone time?" Jordan asked.

"No. Come on out."

They stood side by side, gazing out at the large backyard even though the darkness obscured the details. "Your stars," Jordan said after a while, his gaze tilted toward the sky. "You said there were a ton of them, and you were right."

"It's better if you get a few miles out of town." But he had to admit, the skyscape was beautiful even here.

When he and Jordan got up to his old room and started to unpack, Landry found a surprise. "Pajamas?" he asked, holding up a pair of blue plaid flannel pants.

"Or loungewear."

"I don't own these."

Jordan walked over to land a kiss on his cheek. "You do now."

"Why?"

"'Cause it's colder here than we're used to, and I thought they'd be cozy." He reached into his bag and pulled out a pair in green plaid. "Look! We can be disgustingly matchy-matchy."

It was just too much for Landry. For no reason he could articulate, this one small gesture overwhelmed him, making his heart beat fast and his entire body heat. He sat gracelessly on the bed. "I don't deserve you."

Jordan pushed Landry's legs apart and knelt between them, his knees cushioned by an antique throw rug Landry had won at an auction when he was fourteen. Then Jordan cradled Landry's face in his palms. "You do deserve me. You lost your husband way too soon, but it didn't make you bitter. Elaine says you were an amazing boss, and when she left, you gave her enough money to really live her dream. You gave me a chance at a job even though I had no real experience at it. You never once judged me for mistakes in my past. You bought a car for me to drive, and you let me live at your house. You never acted snooty toward me. You are a kind man who wants the same thing I do—to improve people's lives. You work so hard all the time, but I've never seen you try to gain anything at another person's expense. You deserve happiness, Landry Bishop. You deserve love."

For a long time, Landry stared at him. "May I kiss you?"

There was that Stryker smile, lighting up the room like fireworks. "I wish you would."

So Landry did. First a gentle press of lips to lips, and he didn't hurry, preferring to drink in the sensation of soft skin. After a minute or two, Landry parted his lips, and Jordan followed suit, eagerly accepting Landry's tongue into his mouth. Yes, a slight taste of tuna lingered, but Landry didn't mind. He also tasted the chocolate ice cream and sugared coffee they'd had for dessert, and when he finally lifted his hands to Jordan's head, Landry luxuriated in silky hair against his fingertips.

Then Landry broke the kiss, moving his mouth to the juncture of Jordan's neck and shoulder. Jordan leaned his head back and moaned.

"Are your knees sore yet?" Landry asked.

"I don't care."

Landry puffed laughter against Jordan's neck. "Let's get ready for bed, okay?"

"Spoilsport."

Jordan rose with a slight groan, and then he offered Landry a hand up too. They squeezed into the bathroom across the hall to brush their teeth, jostling each other playfully in front of the sink. Landry skipped his nightly skin-care regime. Back in Landry's room, they undressed and pulled on the flannel pants, tickling each other as they went. At one point Landry lost his balance and swore as he nearly fell on his ass.

"Shh!" Jordan made a show of putting a finger to his lips. "You'll wake the kids."

They climbed into bed together—a double, so it was a tighter squeeze than the king they shared in LA— and Landry doused the light on the nightstand, leaving them in almost complete darkness.

"Have you had another guy in this bed before?" Jordan whispered. They were face-to-face on a single pillow, arms wrapped around each other.

"No."

"So where did you and your youthful flings do the deed? Haystacks and barns?"

"I was a virgin until I got to college."

"Really?"

"Yes. Um... I made out a couple of times with Tim Spohr behind the library, but we never got past first base. He ended up moving to Omaha after we graduated. Don't know what happened to him."

Jordan kissed the tip of his nose. "Tim Spohr's loss."

"How about you?"

"I have also never slept with anyone in this bed."

That made Landry tickle him until they were in danger of growing too noisy. Then Jordan let out a big breath and leaned his forehead on Landry's shoulder. "I was fifteen, which was too young, and he was twenty, which was too old, but he was cute and I thought I knew everything. I mean, it was my idea as much as his, but I was pretty drunk. There was nothing special about it, you know?"

"First times don't have to be special. Mine was in my dorm with some boy from my math class. We had to sexile my roommate first, and I think we lasted about thirty seconds."

More giggles ensued, but they died out as Landry and Jordan allowed their hands to wander over bare chests and backs and then under the loose waistbands of the pants. Soon all the flannel was down past their knees and they were grinding against each other, needy and voracious. Their moans and pleas grew noisy, until Landry decided the best way to silence Jordan was with a kiss.

It worked wonderfully well.

Landry had packed condoms and lube this time. Probably so had Jordan. But that meant getting out of bed, and Landry wasn't willing to break contact for even that long. No matter. It was enough to thrust together, to feel Jordan's strong ass flexing beneath his palms and Jordan's fingers digging into his glutes. The old bedsprings squeaked beneath them. Jordan was so solid against him, so real, so hot and vital and *necessary*.

With some difficulty, Landry squeezed his hand between them and grasped their hard, slick shafts in his fist. That was exactly the extra bit of friction they needed. Their thrusts grew faster and less rhythmic, until Landry muffled a cry against the tender skin of Jordan's neck. But that left Jordan's mouth free, and he called out when he came.

Moments later, breathing hard and still embracing, they heard a toilet flush.

"Do you think we woke someone up?" Jordan whispered.

That set Landry laughing, trying to keep hushed about it but not succeeding, and Jordan joined him. Jordan was still chuckling as Landry drifted to sleep.

IN the morning, neither Missy nor Rod mentioned anything about nocturnal disturbances. But Jordan and Landry kept catching each other's gaze and snickering like naughty schoolboys.

Then Landry saw Jordan deep in discussion with the kids, the subject apparently centering on their overflowing toy box, and a realization slammed him: Jordan was happy. The weariness he'd carried when he first arrived at Landry's door had long since evaporated, replaced with energy and joy. Jordan had turned out to be good at his job—exceptionally good—and his sense of proficiency had obviously been good for his soul. Landry could understand that and was proud to know he'd played a part in helping Jordan find his place in the world. Landry smiled, and when Jordan saw him, his entire face lit up with delight.

Because it was a Saturday, Missy and her family lounged around a bit after breakfast. Landry, though, grew increasingly jumpy, dreading whatever was going to happen at one that afternoon.

"I'm going to the Barn Owl," he finally announced. "Anyone need anything?"

"What's the Barn Owl?" asked Jordan. He was helping the twins build something with oversized Legos.

"Grocery store."

"Can I go?"

"I doubt it'll be exciting, but sure."

They put on shoes and jackets—after Missy peeled the twins off Jordan—said goodbye, and went outside. Down the street, a woman knelt in front of her house, pulling the last of the year's weeds from a flowerbed. She waved at them, and although Landry didn't recognize her, he waved back. Then he got into the truck's driver's seat.

"Hey, Lan? Are we in a hurry?"

"Not especially."

"Then will you give me a tour?"

"Sure. Just don't expect nonstop thrills."

He took them downtown first, where he did a slow complete circle around the town square. A few pedestrians stared curiously at them, and Jordan seemed enchanted by his view from the passenger seat. "It's adorable. Like a movie set."

"What movie would that be?"

"*The Life Story of Landry Bishop.* Oscar bait for sure. Who plays me?"

Landry squeezed Jordan's knee. "Nobody. There's no substitute for you."

After the town square, they rolled around Peril's central neighborhood, where older houses like Missy's were interspersed with smaller ones, some built in the forties and fifties. Landry was surprised to discover that all the homes looked occupied and well tended. Apparently not everyone had fled.

Landry pointed out the schools he'd attended, the DQ, the church his parents had dragged him to a few times a year, and the library.

"Where Tim Spohr almost got lucky," Jordan said.

"Yeah. And where I spent a lot of my free time."

There were newer houses nearer the edge of town. Nice ranch homes—without the ranch but with expansive front yards decorated with wagon wheels, flags, and miniature windmills and tractors. "In case anyone is in danger of forgetting we're in Nebraska," he scoffed.

"Don't be a snob. It's cute."

And then they were driving past fields laid bare for the coming winter and farmsteads with a few dairy cows or a scattering of goats. Those didn't last long either. Landry turned off the highway onto county roads surrounded only by rangeland—curving hills covered in brown grasses, small basins that held water from the last rains, mildly curious cattle watching from afar. And above them an endless sky of faded blue, streaked with a few wispy cirrus clouds.

Eventually Landry circled back toward town, but before they reached Peril, he parked near the railroad tracks. He and Jordan watched as a long coal train snaked its way eastward from Wyoming.

"See?" Landry felt the train rattling deep in his bones. "Not much in the way of sights."

"It was probably really stifling when you were a kid. But I like it. It's… sincere. Besides, traffic's a whole lot better than in LA."

"True."

They sat there long after the train was gone. Silent, holding hands, staring off at the horizon.

Chapter Sixteen

"OH my God, Landry! You look *sharp*!"

Landry looked down at himself and then at Missy. "Is it too much? Am I overdressed?" He wore a brown-and-aqua windowpane sport coat with dark blue trousers and a dress shirt in a blue so pale it was almost white. His silk tie was a slightly psychedelic floral print in a spectrum of blues.

"No, but I'm starting to wonder if I'm underdressed."

"You look fantastic, Miss. Really." She'd never been fond of fancy clothes, and he wondered if she'd bought her pretty black dress especially for this occasion.

The whole family looked their best—Rod in a suit and tie and the twins similarly attired. "I was going to get Bryanna a dress," Missy explained. "But she wanted a suit like Blake's. Good choice, actually. She looks cute."

"She does." He cast Missy a sidelong glance, and she grinned and shrugged. A four-year-old's decision to wear boys' clothes instead of girls' probably said nothing about her sexual orientation or gender identity, but Missy didn't seem to care if it did. Neither did Rod, who proudly took a kid in each hand and posed for Missy's picture-taking.

Jordan was a treat too. He wore his Vegas suit, which looked as if it had been made just for him. He'd brushed his hair back from his face, emphasizing his eyes and jawline. And his smile was at maximum level. "Wow, are we a gorgeous bunch or what? Hollywood ain't got nothin' on us."

Missy took a lot more photos, until Rod pointed out that if they didn't leave, they were going to be late.

"To *what*?" Landry whined.

Missy slugged him—gently. "Hold your horses, Wormy. You'll find out soon enough."

Then, after one last bathroom trip for the kids, they left the house. Missy and her crew got into their SUV, and Landry and Jordan got into the truck with Jordan behind the wheel.

"Do you know where we're going?" Landry asked.

"Yep, but not why. Missy was gonna tell me, but I suck at keeping secrets so I told her she better not."

"You obviously take *Know thyself* seriously."

Jordan gave him a steady look. "I've always known my weaknesses. Just lately I'm getting a better view of my strengths." He started the engine and pulled away from the curb.

They didn't drive far. Jordan slowed to a crawl as they reached downtown, where Landry was astonished

to see all the street-side parking spaces filled and a
steady stream of pedestrians heading in one direction.
"Are all these people—"

"You betcha. You're the only game in town
today, Lan."

Landry's mouth went dry. He yearned desperately
for a cherry limeade from Sonic, a Quarter Pounder,
his Vegas sweats, and a big-screen TV with a season
of *Parks and Recreation* ready to go. He would rather
have done a striptease on *The Tonight Show* than deal
with whatever he was about to face. What version of
the fabulous, famous Landry Bishop was this crowd
expecting? Didn't they realize he was just weird
Wormy, that kid they used to shake their heads at?
What the *hell* had Aunt Trudy done to him?

Landry thought Jordan was going to take them to
the library, but they continued on another half block,
where Aunt Trudy and an assortment of relatives stood
in the driveway of a bright yellow bungalow. The front
yard contained a swarm of people—some standing and
talking, others milling around a sign obscured by a blue
plastic tarp. Aunt Trudy gestured impatiently at Jordan
to pull into the driveway as she herded everyone out of
the way. When Jordan stopped the truck, she hobbled
quickly to the passenger door and yanked it open.
"Hurry! Everyone's waiting for you."

"Why?"

She rolled her eyes with a skill that any teenager
would envy. "Get your butt in gear and you'll see why."

Dutifully Landry unbuckled and climbed out.
"You look really nice, Aunt Trudy. That dress is perfect
for you." It was a caftan with peacock-colored abstract
shapes highlighted by metallic dots and squiggles. On

anyone else it might have been over-the-top, but it matched her bold, quirky personality.

Smiling, she gave the fabric a quick pat. "I've been waiting almost a year to wear it. Now come on."

She led a procession toward the bungalow's front porch, Landry and Jordan behind her and a phalanx of family buffering Landry from what seemed to be the entire population of Peril.

"You okay?" Jordan whispered.

Landry nodded and took his hand.

A wide, rainbow-striped ribbon blocked the house's front door, and a strange delegation waited for them on the porch—middle-aged men and women in conservative, churchgoing clothes, plus a cluster of more creatively attired teenagers. One of the boys wore eyeliner and had purple stripes in his hair; he covered his mouth and bounced up and down as Landry came near.

People continued to file into the front yard, soon overflowing onto the sidewalk and adjacent properties. Various folks shook Landry's hand, apparently including the mayor and city council—one member of which he vaguely remembered as his high school English teacher. She hugged him and told him how proud she was of him, although she didn't say why. The kids introduced themselves too, the eyeliner boy so nervous and giggly that he could barely speak. Aunt Trudy watched all the interactions with a smug smile.

The mayor snagged Landry and began a monologue on Peril's recent economic growth, which didn't seem to have much to do with anything, but Landry nodded politely. After a few minutes Aunt Trudy tapped her cane against the mayor's leg. "Can it, Norm. You're not campaigning today. Let's get this show going."

Mayor Norm smiled sheepishly and shut up.

A thin woman handed him a cordless microphone. It took him a moment to figure out how to turn it on, and then he spent some time tapping it and saying "testing, testing." Apparently satisfied it was working, he finally began. "Welcome, Peril!" he boomed. The speakers shrieked with feedback, but at least everyone stopped talking and turned toward the porch.

"Welcome!" Mayor Norm repeated but in a more moderate voice. "And thank you all for making the trek to our beautiful downtown on this fine Saturday afternoon. It's a great pleasure to see so many of you here. I'm going to turn the mic over in a second, but first I'm supposed to remind you that after the ceremony, you should all head over to the community center, where we'll have cookies, coffee, and punch. Sponsored by the fine folks of Ethel's Eats and Svoboda Ranch and Home!"

He paused for a round of applause. The residents of Peril seemed excited at the prospect of a snack.

"And now let me hand things over to the woman who made this all possible, Trudy Bishop-Tucker!"

Nobody in the history of the world had looked more comfortable with a mic in her hand than Aunt Trudy. She held it with the confidence of a veteran performer, and she faced the crowd with an expression of supreme satisfaction. But before she said a word, she motioned imperiously at Landry, ordering him to stand at her side. He wondered if the crowd could tell how baffled he was.

"I was born right here in Peril," Aunt Trudy began. "So were my parents and my grandparents. My great-grandparents came here in 1883. We've been around here near as long as the town itself. And you know what? In all those years, us Perilians have mostly kept to ourselves. We're like a secret, and there's a lot of us who like it that way."

Enthusiastic clapping and cheers sounded in response.

"But even if we're happy to be undiscovered, I guess we don't mind a little fame rubbing off on us now and then. Earl Humphrey was from Peril, and he was one of the most important photographers of the early twentieth century. Our late congressman, LeRoy Redfield, he was from here. So was Helen Cooper, one of the first female radio broadcasters in Nebraska."

Landry had heard of these people. Their names got trotted out regularly during his school years, usually accompanied by grainy black-and-white photos. But he still had no idea how he was involved.

After a dramatic pause, Aunt Trudy continued. "But you know what? In all the history of this town, we've never had *two* world-famous Perilians at the same time. But that's what we have now."

Ah. Landry shifted uncomfortably while trying to maintain a bland smile.

"Now, one of our boys, you all know about him. Jaxon Powers. I'm not a big fan of his music, but he sure did us proud, didn't he? A genuine hero!" Wild applause. "And when he was done being a hero, he came home and gave a nice fat donation to our schools." Even *wilder* applause. Landry joined in because he thought it was fantastic that Powers had decided to support art education in Peril. Some kids found their place in sports or academics, but for many of them, the drama club or marching band proved their real chance to shine, to feel pride in themselves.

Aunt Trudy clapped Landry's shoulder a few times. "Our *other* famous boy, I'm so proud to say, is my own nephew, Landry Bishop. I think a lot of us folks remember when he was growing up, how he'd help out with decorating at various functions. He used to go through the mail-order catalogs with some of us to help us pick out clothing and furniture. Remember that?"

Oh God. Landry's cheeks flamed. People must have thought him a bossy little twit, way too pretentious for his place.

And yet everyone in the crowd cheered and clapped, and if there was derision or irony in their actions, he couldn't find it.

Aunt Trudy tapped him again. "Landry hasn't had the chance to save a country yet. But he has always had the courage to be true to himself, to show us all who he really is, even when that was a really hard thing to do. Sure, he had the support of his family, but that didn't mean he didn't struggle. I love this town, but places like Peril don't always appreciate the kind of special our Landry has."

He was going to stop her. This was ridiculous. He wasn't brave or special, and he didn't deserve to have this kind of attention.

But Aunt Trudy ignored his pleading look. "After Landry graduated high school, he showed his bravery again. He went all the way to California on his own, at an age when a lot of kids can't make it to the Barn Owl without finding trouble. He graduated college summa cum laude. And then he made a household name for himself—not by being the most outrageous or by squirming his way into the gossip columns, but by giving everyday people tips on making their lives brighter, more fun, more charming, more organized. And he's been an inspiration to so many, showing folks how they can achieve their dreams and still remain humble."

Landry touched his cheek and realized he was crying. He hadn't known that anyone but Jordan thought of him this way—not even his own family.

He'd thought all of Peril considered him that weird gay kid who ran off to make a career out of frivolities. But now all of these people were beaming at him, calling his name, and the eyeliner boy was crying too.

With a true sense of timing, Aunt Trudy waited until the din had faded just enough. Then she lifted her arms to silence everyone. "Our Landry has been through hardships. He's lost too many people who loved him, way too soon. But he's also a true example of how much our youths can achieve just by being their real, beautiful selves."

He really wished he had a hanky. Or at least a tissue. But then, as if by magic, Jordan pressed a Kleenex into Landry's hand. Landry dabbed at his eyes.

"Today couldn't have happened without the support of the mayor, the city council, the Peril school district, many of our local businesses, and—most importantly—you, the people of Peril. And it is with great pleasure that today we can officially open the Landry Bishop Center for Youth Diversity."

While Landry gaped and the audience erupted even louder than before, somebody pulled the tarp off the sign. Lettered both front and back, the sign sported the center's name in rainbow-hued letters, and a brown hand clasped a peach-toned one. It was colorful, cheerful. Welcoming.

But Aunt Trudy wasn't finished. "This center will serve as a haven for children and teenagers anywhere along the LGBTQI spectrum and their allies, as well as any young people in Peril who feel the need for community and acceptance and who want to build their unique strengths and make their voices heard. The center will provide counseling, education, leadership training, fellowship, and safe haven. We want every youngster in Peril to know they have value."

After another round of raucous applause died down, Aunt Trudy turned to Landry. "Would you like to say anything, dear?"

Shit. How was he supposed to speak when his eyes swam with tears and his throat was tight with emotion? But he took the mic, wiped his eyes, and cleared his throat.

"Um... I don't have a prepared speech. Mostly because until right now I had no idea what was going on. It's no wonder the town is a secret—you all are really good at being hush-hush."

Everyone laughed, which helped ease his tension.

"Anyway, I'm going to keep this short because you're all raring to get at those cookies. I just want to say how... well, honored doesn't even touch on how I feel. This might be the most amazing thing that has ever happened to me. It is so wonderful that Peril's kids will have this place, especially because the center will be a big reminder to every one of them that Peril cares. That's the best thing you can do for your children— love them for who they are."

He took a deep breath and shot a quick smile at Jordan, who looked a little damp-eyed too. "I'm not going to lie to you. However much you accept them, some of your kids are going to leave Peril, just like I did. Maybe their best futures lie in Lincoln or New York or Tokyo. But when you build a place like this center, they know that no matter what, they'll always have a home in Peril. Thank you all for giving them this precious gift."

And that was all he could manage, but it seemed to satisfy the crowd. Landry exchanged hugs with Aunt

Trudy, Missy and her gang, an assortment of relatives, and everyone on the porch. Then someone handed him a pair of those silly oversize scissors, which Landry used to cut the ribbon across the door.

It took some time and a lot more hand-shaking, but eventually Landry got to enter the house. A young woman who introduced herself as Molly, the center's director, led him on a tour—with stops for the *Peril Gazette* reporter to snap photos. The center boasted a large lounge area filled with comfortable furniture and a big-screen TV, complete with gaming system. The kitchen had been outfitted with commercial appliances, and all the rooms met ADA accessibility standards. There was office space as well as rooms that could be used for classes, meetings, or counseling sessions. Overall, the décor was bright and optimistic.

Down in the basement, Molly waved at empty desks and bookshelves. "We're still gathering donations for this part, but we hope to have computers so the kids can do homework or write, plus a nice collection of diverse YA fiction."

"Would a hundred thousand dollars fill those needs?"

Molly and the rest of the small group gasped, and Aunt Trudy took his arm. "You have no obligation to do this, Lan. We named it after you to honor you, not extort you."

Landry didn't regret his instinctive offer. "I'm not feeling bullied. I'd just really like to help."

Molly surprised him with a fierce hug. "I can't tell you how much this means to us."

Eventually the tour ended. Landry signed autographs for a few people and posed with them, including the boy with the eyeliner. "I love your hair color," Landry said as he scribbled his name on the flyleaf of one of his books. "It looks fantastic on you, and whoever did it did a great job."

A girl poked the boy until he spoke. "I, um, did it myself."

"And mine too!" said the girl, whose hair was shades of aqua. "Plus he painted this amazing mural in my bedroom. Oh my God, it's so fantastic! Look!" She pulled out her phone, scrolled frantically, and then handed it to Landry.

Even though the photos weren't great quality, Landry could tell that the artwork was beautiful and creative—a swirl of abstract shapes and bright hues that perfectly conveyed youthfulness and joy.

"Wow!" Landry exclaimed. "I love it. I hope you're considering a career as an artist." He handed the phone back to the beaming girl.

The boy lifted his chin. "I'm applying to art schools in California and Chicago." He looked determined and proud and a little frightened.

Landry handed him the book and set a hand on his shoulder. "I'm going to be hoping you achieve everything you dream of. If you need an extra letter of recommendation, drop me an email. Jordan screens my emails, so just remind him you're from Peril and I'll see what I can do to help."

The boy nearly strangled Landry with the force of his embrace.

Right at that moment, Landry didn't crave fast food, cheap comfy clothes, or escapist TV. Right now he had everything he wanted.

Chapter Seventeen

LANDRY had to go to the community center and pose for photos and eat bland grocery store cookies. He didn't mind too much. It was interesting to chat with some of the people he'd grown up with. Even the ones who'd treated him badly back then seemed genuinely thrilled to see him again. He didn't carry grudges. Being young was hard, and with the perspective of maturity, he knew many of those people had carried burdens of their own. He even suspected that the adversity he'd faced while young had helped him grow strong.

He had no idea how long the socializing might stretch on. Missy and her family had left some time ago, when the twins got too excited and tired and teetered on the verge of tantrums. Landry was just beginning to flag when Jordan approached and said, in a louder voice than necessary, "Landry, we have to go. You have that Skype meeting with Ms. Winfrey, remember?"

Well, nobody could argue with that. After a few final hugs, Jordan bundled Landry into the truck. But instead of heading back to their house, where dinner needed preparing, Jordan drove out of town and stopped again at the railroad tracks. No trains were passing now.

"Oh my God," Landry said after a long silence.

"Yeah."

"That was…. Oh my God."

"I love how authors like you have such an extensive vocabulary." Jordan squeezed Landry's knee. "But you're right. Oh my God."

That seemed to about cover it, so they stayed quiet for several minutes. But then Jordan cocked his head. "Do you really have a hundred grand to toss around like that?"

"I've been thinking about the Jag, just sitting in the garage and gathering dust. Since it was a gift from Steve and selling it could provide the bulk of the donation money, I was maybe going to ask them to dedicate the library to him. If that's okay with you."

"Why wouldn't it be okay with me?"

"Because now that we're together, I don't want—"

Jordan stopped him with a raised hand. "He was your husband and you loved him. I'm not jealous of him, Lan. I think it'd be really nice for you to honor his memory that way."

"Jesus." Landry shook his head in wonderment. "You are one amazing human being, Jordan Stryker."

Level ten smile. "Do you know the moment I started falling in love with you?"

"Love?"

"Yep. L-O-V-E. Maybe some people might say this is too fast, that we haven't known each other very long, but they'd be wrong. There's the click, remember? Plus I've been waiting thirty years for you. That's plenty long enough."

Landry moved in for a kiss, but Jordan held him off. "Nope, not yet. I was telling you something. The moment, right? When I saw the light?"

"Okay, when was that?"

"Do you remember that awful dinner I made? With the gross sauces and seasonings?"

Landry chuckled. "It was pretty unforgettable."

"Kind of like the Hindenburg disaster. I thought you were gonna fire me. But you didn't even yell. You didn't make me feel like a huge fuckup. You were just, *Oh well, shit happens, let's clean up and eat sandwiches*."

"That made you fall in love with me?"

"Start to, yeah. 'Cause you acted like I could fail without being a failure. A few days later you smiled at me over breakfast. And that…." He paused and cleared his throat. "That did it."

Landry's throat felt thick too. "I haven't told you this enough, but you're remarkable, Jordan. You haven't just made my everyday life easier, although you've accomplished that as well. You've also helped me see myself more clearly. Helped me become a better version of myself."

"I…." Jordan sniffed loudly. His eyes might have been a little dewy, but his smile could have illuminated all of Nebraska. When he spoke, his voice rasped slightly. "Good. Some people used to tell me I lacked ambition, but I didn't. I dreamed of making a difference to someone. I'm so glad that someone is you." They did kiss then. They made out like teenagers, actually, not even stopping when a passing train shook the truck. And just as the train disappeared into the distance, Landry reached a decision.

Chapter Eighteen

LANDRY hadn't made it to the Barn Owl the previous day, and going today meant stopping every three feet to shake someone's hand and thank them for their congratulations. He was pleased, however, to discover that the store had improved its selection since he'd moved away, and he was able to find some surprisingly exotic groceries. Well, exotic for Peril. He wondered who in town regularly consumed kimchi, matcha, and hummus.

After changing into jeans and a sweater, he got to work in the kitchen. The twins were napping, and Jordan was helping Rod assemble a new storage system in the garage. Missy sat on a kitchen chair and watched Landry prep.

"How are you doing? After the extravaganza, I mean." She looked slightly worried.

"I'm still pretty overwhelmed." The dried porcini mushrooms had already rehydrated in a bowl of water, and now he drained them and began to chop. He smiled when he realized the knife was part of the set he'd sent Missy and Rod for Christmas a few years earlier.

"It was quite a to-do," she agreed. "You sure held up well, though. I can't imagine standing there and talking to all those people without even note cards to rely on."

"I still can't believe Aunt Trudy did that. I mean the center itself—that's incredible. But naming it after me?"

"We're proud of you, Wormy."

He smiled at her. "I'm proud of you too. Rod, the twins, everything you've done with this house…. You've done well for yourself. You have a really great family. And you've always, always had my back."

Her chin wobbled, and she sniffled. She reached for a paper napkin, mumbling something improbable about allergies before she blew her nose.

And he winked at her and smiled, because he'd already cried once today, and that was more than enough.

HE popped dinner in the oven just as Rod and Jordan tromped in from the garage, both of them happily smudged with dust. Rod sniffed the air. "Wow, smells good! What're you making?"

"Lasagna."

"Really? I love lasagna. I was sort of expecting something schmancier, though."

"It has celery root, mushrooms, and a white sauce."

Rod grinned. "See? Schmancy! Can't wait."

"You'll have to wait about an hour for it to bake."

"Perfect, 'cause we've gotta wash up." He held aloft a pair of filthy hands.

While Rod and Jordan went upstairs to clean up—
Jordan first detouring to kiss Landry's cheek—Missy
disappeared to investigate the ominous bangs coming
from Blake's room. And that was perfect for Landry,
who grabbed his phone and ducked outside onto the
back porch. Ignoring the chill and gazing out at the
frost-killed garden and the tree he'd once fallen out of,
he called Suzee.

Just as Landry reentered the kitchen, Jordan came in
too, all tidied up and with his hair slightly damp. Landry
wanted to drag him upstairs to bed but instead took his
hand. "Would you go for a short drive with me?"

"Sure! Need more mushrooms?"

"No, this is something else."

They grabbed their jackets, and Landry found Rod
in the living room, picking up toys. "Can you do me a
favor? If the oven buzzes before we're back, just turn
the temperature down to two hundred."

"Sure." Rod dumped an armful of action figures
into a toy chest. "Two hundred."

Landry got behind the wheel this time, and Jordan
didn't ask where they were headed. Maybe he could tell
from the tightness of Landry's shoulders that patience
was best. Landry headed south out of town, but not by
far. No other cars were in sight when he parked at the
side of the road.

"Cemetery?" Jordan asked.

"Yes."

Without further comment, Landry led him down a
familiar path to a granite stone engraved with two names
and sets of dates. The last time he'd visited, there had been
only one. "I should have brought flowers," he said.

Jordan stood close against him. "We can come
back later if you want."

"Maybe." Perhaps he should have felt sad, standing at his parents' plot, but he didn't, not really. Partly because he'd finished mourning them long ago, and partly because the decisions he'd made this afternoon felt so right. He was a little nervous, yet more comfortable in his skin than he could remember. His parents would have been happy to know that.

"Do you see all the Bishops?" Landry asked.

Jordan took a few minutes to wander around. "Wow. They're everywhere."

"Yes. We've been dropping dead around here for well over a century."

"Impressive. And it's a nice cemetery."

"It's better in the summer, when the trees have leaves. But yes." Landry pointed to an empty space close to his parents' grave. "That plot is mine."

"Seriously?"

"Completely. My grandfather bought it in my name right after I was born."

Jordan walked over to the space and looked down at the dry grass. "Isn't that kind of creepy?"

"I thought so at first. But my dad said *his* dad was just making sure I'd have a spot close to everyone else for my final rest. Still morbid, but also sort of sweet."

"It is." Jordan chuckled. "The more I learn about your family, the more I like them."

"I was thinking…. Steve wanted to be cremated. His relatives are a bunch of homophobic shitheads who didn't even bother to show up for the memorial service, so I don't care about them. And I never knew quite what to do with the ashes, so… they're in the closet in my study. Top shelf. Now I'm thinking maybe I should inter them here."

Jordan wrapped an arm around Landry's waist. "I think that's a really nice idea."

"Good. But believe it or not, I didn't drag you out here to discuss Steve or the legion of deceased Bishops." Landry detached himself so he could face Jordan.

"You look very serious." Jordan bit his lip and shifted his stance uneasily.

"That's because I'm going to have to let you go."

"I…. What?"

"I don't need a PA anymore. I turned down Suzee's offer. In fact, I've decided to stop doing any live appearances. I'm going to concentrate on my books and my blog."

Jordan answered in a whisper. "Why?"

"Because that's what I really want to do. A wise woman once told me, and I quote, 'Be more of who you want to be instead of who you think you should be.' I want to stop trying to fit some image and instead be the real Landry Bishop. Not the brand, but a man from Nebraska who gives pretty good advice about how to turn your bedroom into a relaxing retreat."

For good reason, Jordan looked confused and shaken. Yet he managed a genuine smile. "That's great, Landry. I'm so glad for you."

"It *feels* great. Like a huge weight is gone."

"You look… I don't know. Loose? Grounded. Was there something specific that helped you make this decision?"

Landry reached up to give Jordan's cheek a quick stroke. "You helped. But also I noticed something after we got here. People were making a huge fuss over me, but they weren't hounding me with questions about which stars I know or how glamorous life is in Hollywood. They were telling me things instead—about their kids, their jobs, their psoriasis." He chuckled. "I could have lived without that last topic. Anyway, I realized they were all saying the same thing, and today at the center, they really drove that message home."

"And what was that?" Jordan asked quietly.

"They *want* me. Not because I'm famous, but because I'm me. In their hearts, I never stopped being a Perilian. I guess maybe in my heart, I never stopped either."

"Are you planning to move here?"

Landry laughed and shook his head. "That's a step too far. But I'll visit. I'll do a better job of keeping in touch. And when I die, well, I guess I'll come home for good." He scraped his foot across his waiting burial plot.

Jordan nodded. "But you don't need a PA anymore."

"Not really. I won't be flying off to New York or making appointments with designers. I won't be working all the time."

Again, an authentic smile from Jordan. "I'm really glad to hear that. And I totally understand. I'll find another job—I always do. But what about us? The personal us, not professional."

This next part was tricky. Dangerous, maybe. But Landry wanted it more than anything. "Actually, I'm laying you off as PA, but I have another position to offer you instead."

"Yeah?" A hint of a smile played at the edges of Jordan's lips, and his eyes held a definite sparkle. "What position is that?"

Landry dropped onto one knee. Fortunately his gravesite was soft. "Partner. Life partner. I, uh, don't have a ring to offer you at the moment. But will you consider a position as my husband?"

Stryker Scale level ten. No. Eleven.

Jordan whooped loud enough to scare some birds from a nearby tree. Then he grabbed Landry by the biceps, hauled him to his feet, and crushed him in a bear hug. "Yes!" he whispered into Landry's ear. "Yes, and yes!"

And dammit, now Landry *was* crying again. "You didn't even wait to hear my complete offer."

"I don't care. This position comes with benefits way too good to pass up." Jordan squeezed him even harder. "Besides, will my job description really change all that much? PA or husband, I'll still be the guy who helps you be the very best Landry you can be. That's the best job in the world."

"And I get to help you be the world's best Jordan. We'll work together to be a spectacular us."

Kissing one's fiancé passionately atop one's own burial plot might have been unusual, but Landry had the sense that none of the surrounding Bishops would disapprove. Somebody drove by, honking long and loud and interrupting the mood for the moment.

"Are we going to stay in LA?" Jordan asked.

Landry had given this a bit of thought. "We could, if you wanted. But there's no reason we have to. We can live wherever we like."

"You'd give up your beautiful house? The pool? The view?"

"The traffic. The pretension. The incessant sunshine." Landry loved his house, but he could easily love another as long as Jordan was there to share it. And considering the asking price for a Hollywood Hills mansion, he'd be able to afford just about anything somewhere else.

"Seattle doesn't have incessant sunshine." Jordan's eyes glittered with excitement.

"And it has a good foodie scene, plus some homes with lovely views. I think I'd enjoy Seattle." Landry caught Jordan's hand and kissed the back of it. "Whither thou goest, I will go. Where thou lodgest, I will lodge."

"Are you going to write a blog on how to romance your fiancé with Old Testament verses?"

"There you go. You're in your new position for two minutes and already you're helping me."

That led to another kiss, this one as good as the last and promising many more in the future.

"We'd better get back to your lasagna," Jordan said with a pat to Landry's ass.

"And to share our good news."

Jordan took Landry's hand and they began to walk back to the truck. "We have to call Elaine right away," Jordan said.

"Of course. I'd like to ask her to be my best woman." She could even wear that dress he'd brought her from New York, if she wanted. "Um, do you suspect she may have been—"

"Trying to set us up? I've been thinking that for a while." Jordan whooped another loud laugh. "Good old Elaine. She's going to think it's funny you popped the question in a cemetery in Nebraska."

"Are you kidding? Marriage proposals in rural graveyards are the latest thing. Landry Bishop says so."

"Well, if Landry Bishop says so…."

Laughing, teasing, giddy from pure joy, Landry and Jordan got into the truck and began their journey together.

Coming in June 2019

Dreamspun Desires #83
The More the Merrier by Sean Michael

Too much of a good thing?

When Logan gets the call about newborn triplets in need of a home, he steps up, realizing too late the daunting task he's taken on. He'd be lost without the men of the Teddy Bear Club—especially Dirk.

He even offers to spend spring break at Logan's home, helping him and the babies settle in. Dirk loves being a dad, and he wants to help Logan find the same joy. It doesn't hurt that they enjoy spending time together.

Before they even realize it, they're settling into a routine... becoming a family.

Falling in love.

But their new bond is about to face the ultimate test. Will they come through and realize that with love, there's no such thing as enough?

Dreamspun Desires #84
Fake Dating the Prince by Ashlyn Kane

A royal deception. An accidental romance.

When fast-living flight attendant Brayden Wood agrees to accompany a first-class passenger to a swanky charity ball, he discovers his date—"Call me Flip"—is actually His Royal Highness Prince Antoine-Philipe. And he wants Brayden to pretend to be his boyfriend.

Being Europe's only prince with an Indian parent—and its only *openly* gay one—has led Flip to select "appropriate" men first and worry about attraction later. Still, flirty, irreverent Brayden captivates him right away, and Flip needs a date to survive the ball without being match-made.

Before Flip can pursue Brayden in earnest, the paparazzi forces his hand, and the charade is extended for the remainder of Brayden's vacation.

Posh, gorgeous, thoughtful Prince Flip is way out of Brayden's league. If Brayden survives three weeks of platonically sharing a bed with him during the romantic holiday season, going home afterward might break his heart....